Tales of the Forthcoming:
An Anthology of Science-
fiction and Supernatural Short
Stories

by Steven Blows

Edited by Pauline Nolet

Cover Design by
THISISREALLYCHRIS

ISBN: 978-1-0685243-0-1

Acknowledgements

Before I begin, a quick *hello!* to anyone who knows me.

I would like to thank my friends and family for their unwavering support, which without, I would not have the time and space to put pen to paper.

I would like to give a special thanks (in no particular order) to Cristina Passalacqua, Paul Hounsell, and Thomas Blows. These three are my first line of defence in the arduous challenge of rewriting. No matter what genre or form of writing I present them with, their insights are sure to strike me with inspiration and lead to a renewed excitement. Without Cristina's energetic cheerleading, Paul's simple yet profound perspective, and Thomas's natural inclination of what makes a story entertaining, I would not have the stories that I present you with today. Thanks to Paul, the story "Unbeknownst" has gone from being the shortest to the longest in the collection.

I would also like to thank Liam Cairns for offering some early feedback allowing for this book to head in the right direction.

Thanks for everything,

Steven

Contents

The Orb of King Wallace

A flicker of a match briefly lit what was in front of me. Darkness. I touched the match with my torch, and the room became clear. Light tried its best to fight the blackness, but even so this place was dismal enough that a bottom-dwelling torkan wouldn't cross it on its most daring of days. I was no longer standing in the hallway I had been in seconds before. Instead, I found myself in a small room half full of water and half full of the skeletons of previous victims of this trap. The smell was worse than rotten mildew mixed with ammonia.

I pushed against each of the four walls, hoping to nudge one out of place or perhaps find a crevice on their surfaces for a stable foothold to climb. Neither of these solutions presented themselves, but what did happen was far worse than the twenty-foot drop I had just experienced. The walls started to move in towards me. I forced myself to replace panic with confidence. Panic gets you killed. I waited.

The walls moved slowly. At first only a few centimetres a second, but once the old cogs had rid themselves of decades' worth of dust, the walls' speed increased to a few inches per second and then even faster. The ten-foot-square room quickly shrank to nine, then eight, seven, six... yet I waited. My leg bounced on the spot, asking for action. I sprang, jumping into the air, stretching my arms and legs out as I went, latching onto two opposite walls.

With the torch clenched between my teeth, I scurried

up the wall, carefully moving both legs up in unison, quickly followed by my arms. The fire of the torch was too close to my face for comfort and attempted to singe my eyebrows as it licked my neck with its burning caress. I reached the top of the chamber and pulled myself up onto the safe floor above at the exact moment the walls slammed against each other below, crushing the previous victims' bones all over again.

I lay there thinking about the two near-death experiences I had already faced in my quest to claim the most prized possession of King Wallace's tomb, the Orb. Everything – anything – would be worth it once I got my hands on it.

I stood up and continued walking the hallway. I rubbed the burn on my neck as I cursed at the need to use a primitive light source as a result of the electric-pulse-triggered sensors scattered throughout the tomb. I shouldn't complain. The punishment of a burn is far less than the certain death guaranteed when failing to abide by the king's rules.

King Wallace had been a smart man and had taken every precaution to stop those unworthy from stealing his life's work. Thieves, grave robbers and desperate men had fallen victim to gruesome deaths, but these men were nothing like me. I'd devoted years to planning for the challenge, and I wouldn't let failure enter my sights.

Like I said, King Wallace was a smart man, but not a

selfish man. He would share the Orb with the one who proved their worth by overcoming all the dangers of his tomb and receiving it from his place of eternal dwelling. Everyone must have expected such a precious item, symbolising the power that it does, to be protected by electric fields, laser beams and steel doors. They were wrong and had paid the price. King Wallace was a man of tradition, and I knew his tomb would follow suit, having traps made of string and stone.

The path ahead came to its end against a wall covered in ivy vines. I peeled away the vines, revealing a twelve-digit square panel of turning dials with a lever next to it, indicating its use as an entry key for the code. The gold-plated dials reflected the orange flame of my torch. Each dial was a flat square and had two faces. One face showed an engraved image of a zigzag with a rising sun above it; the other displayed two mountains with the moon sinking behind them.

These symbols were hieroglyphics from the planet Sylia, a planet now long consumed by its growing red star, which would one day turn supernova and paint the night sky with colours to inspire generations of poets.

The symbol of the sun rising above the waves represented the climb of King Wallace to power, and the moon fading behind the mountains represented his fall at the battle of Highlands, but what was the sequence the lock demanded? I stood there thinking, stressfully aware that I was getting no closer to an answer. The lever poking out of the wall mocked me like one schoolboy sticking their tongue out, taunting another.

With nothing else to do, I began to turn the dials, half inspecting them, half playing with them, and fully hoping something would happen. The dials creaked as they moved. I stopped the dials in a random sequence. A good enough try for someone who hasn't got a clue. I pulled the lever. A dull click echoed from within the wall, then silence.

Suddenly, I was startled by something falling from the ceiling above. I jumped backwards, ready to parry an attack that never arrived. Before me hung a shrivelled head tethered to a thick rope made from human hair. The rope came from a small opening in the ceiling above, with two more openings on either side.

I laughed out loud, feeling embarrassed by my actions of being startled by nothing more than a grotesque dungeon ornament, but the message the skull signified struck me still. I had two more chances to enter the correct sequence.

I unpacked my backpack until I located the manuscript of the speech King Wallace gave on his coronation day. I held the torch close as if doing so would cause the paper to reveal a hidden clue. The paper had browned with age and was on the verge of falling apart; thankfully it'd been carefully kept for a number of centuries by the brothers at the monastery until, that is, it was unashamedly misappropriated by myself.

I read the passage until I came to inspiration: "with every sunset, there comes a sunrise". That was it! It had to be it. King Wallace had stayed in power because he planned ahead. With his enemies constantly spying on him, he had to be careful with protecting vital information. He'd released so much fake information that it would swamp the truth. This dial followed the same principle. Twelve dials to trick people into thinking the code was long and complicated, but much like life, if looked at with a different perspective, it can be quick and simple.

I flipped the first dial to show the moon and the second dial to show the sunrise and followed this pattern through to the end. I pulled the lever. The clanking of the cogs released the invisible hand tight around my chest. I sighed in relief. The door slid to the side, and I walked through into the room beyond.

The flame of my torch lit what was close to me. There were two parallel lines of still liquid on the floor, stretching from one end of the room and fading away into the blackness ahead. A potent and distinctive smell of oil seeped into my nostrils. I placed a flame onto each line of oil, and the room burst with light. I dropped my torch to the ground.

The room stretched long and wide, opening a space large enough to fit a king's coffin and all his desired riches. In the centre of the room proudly stood a pyramid holding up King Wallace's coffin. The remaining room was filled with bars of gold piled in their hundreds, an amount so enormous the room gleamed a golden hue. Multiple one-of-a-kind battle armours rested on their stands, waiting for a war they would never fight. Jewels larger than my skull lay stuck behind glass displays. Silver and bronze coins scattered on every inch of floor space, scraping against each other as I walked over them. It all meant nothing to me. I was here for the Orb.

I started my way towards the coffin. As I grew closer to the pyramid, so grew a deep sense of horror of the situation. King Wallace had total undivided control over the Orb, amalgamating years of research to the one solid goal of living forever, yet he'd still ended up helpless and afraid. What chance had I of using its power?

I stopped at the base of the pyramid, gazing upwards at the long stretch of stairs leading its way to the coffin perched at the highest place in the room. I walked the path one step at a time. Once halfway up, I was high enough to see the room from a vantage point. Now, instead of noticing the expensive treasures, I viewed the room itself, or rather the cave itself, for that was what it was. Undoubtedly a man-made cave reclaimed by nature. Long vines dangled from the rocks above, and algae spanned across the ceiling in spotted patches of dark green.

As I placed my foot onto the next step, it let out a

small hiss and sank. Every step of the pyramid simultaneously snapped to a slanted angle in line with the flat surface of the pyramid's face. With no support, gravity claimed me as its own and dragged me down. I sharply grabbed the rock axe strapped onto my leg and drove it deep into the rock with a hefty blow. The axe had a sturdy hold, stopping my fall. I unstrapped another rock axe and, for the second time, started to ascend the pyramid.

The climb was agony. With no natural fight-or-flight reaction to rely on, I pushed forward with raw motivation. Something my body was running dangerously low of. I pulled myself onto the platform at the top of the pyramid. My arms burned with lactic acid. I would have surely failed if the pyramid were any taller, but the past is to be forgotten, and the future is to be lived. I stepped forward.

The coffin lay before me, longer than twelve feet due to the king's tall stature. There were markings on a stone plaque dug into the coffin's lid. It read, "Power comes to those who can take and keep a hold of it". I ran a hand over the stone lid, my fingers bobbling over the engraving. It was beautiful.

I shoved my crowbar under the lid and wrenched the blasted thing off with all the might I had left. The heavy lid hit the floor with a dense bang, shattering the unlucky tiles it landed on. The body inside had decomposed long ago. In its place lay the skeleton of

King Wallace. Its thinness conveyed no hints of the mighty muscles it once wore. The skeleton's arms were crossed, clenching the Orb in their tight grasp. The Orb's light was as magnificent as the stories promised. Its blue-white light danced elegant shadows on the surrounding walls.

I respectfully removed the king's hands and slowly took the item into my right hand. The Orb grew brighter. Its light ominously looking natural and unnatural at the same time. Small clouds whirled around in the Orb's interior. Something was alive in there. A figure burst forth from the Orb, projected in the same illuminating chilled blue light as the Orb itself. It was King Wallace. He appeared wearing light armour shaped under a long ceremonial gown. I fought my instincts to drop the Orb, but held tight and stayed on guard, ready for anything. The projection proceeded to talk in a loud commanding voice, repeated as it bounced along the cave walls.

The projection of King Wallace said, "I praise you, weary adventurer, for the perils you have overcome to stand before me. You have great promise in displaying some of the finest qualities that I show pride on, yet this may not be enough. Now comes the part you cannot escape, the part where your very soul is judged for all its worth."

Light and an invisible force emanated from the Orb. The power was intense and coursed through my body before returning to its source. The king spoke. "I see pride and unladened ego. Do you think you are worthy of holding such an artifact?"

The king's stare was hard to match, but I dared to shy away, knowing that I was worthy. Then, with a graceful nod of his head, he was sucked back into the Orb.

I stood gazing at the power in my hand. *My* power. Thoughts of future conquests flashed in my mind. I was in awe until reality struck me like a spark of electricity. Well, maybe that was because it was a spark of electricity that struck me. Within an instant, my arm holding the Orb was gone. Flesh floated gaily as ash to the floor. The Orb returned of its own accord to its king's possession. A primal fear set in and was released as a screaming howl. I had been judged, and I had been deemed unworthy. I fell to the floor. The tomb's door slammed shut. All light vanished. My screaming continued.

Family Dinner & Troubling Times

"These are troubling times," I say to Kamania as she applies lipstick, partly absent to the world she is inhabiting. The red lipstick strikes an attractive contrast with her light green skin.

I express myself again. "These are troubling times. What with the Anti-Aliens Revelation destroying that Flinakian starship. Over three thousand souls lost!"

"It's appalling. Thank goodness it's light years across the galaxy," Kamania says as she puts down the expensive lipstick worth every credit on her.

"W-what if your brother thinks it was me?" I'm hysterical and must look insane. "What if he thinks I used a warp transporter, teleported to the Nuwey System, flying the flag of Stars and Stripes over countless floating corpses."

Kamania rolls her eyes. I definitely look insane.

"I know, I know, but he might group me in with those horrid people. Humans are the only species stubborn enough to kill. I'm human, and now I'm going to meet your parents for the first time and tell them that we're moving to Earth next rotation. Earth. You know, the home of humans. Forgive me if I seem just a little bit on edge."

"You're not some *human*, you're Jean-Luca Knight, the man I'm going to marry." We stare into each other's eyes, searching for meaning beyond words, beyond worlds. Her black irises reflect my frivolous face.

"Time is getting on. We must leave." Kamania turns.

The smell of her coconut shampoo wafts as she walks past me.

"Hang on. You have something in your hair."

I gently grasp her long hair, combing it through with my fingers, careful not to pull at the sensitive pain cells in Cecian hair. My index finger hits something—

"Ow!" Kamania complains.

"Sorry." I remove the item from her deep red hair. "Just a bit of shampoo." I drop the piece of coconut into her hand and I'm rewarded with a kiss on the cheek. I wonder what a whole coconut would get me.

Kamania enters the passcode into the front gate's security pad. Her parents are smart to take security precautions to protect what they've earned. It makes sense, especially when there are humans around.

The gate opens to reveal a house of architectural wonder. The house is a muddle of materials and a mixture of designs, yet against all logical outlooks, it works. The house displays the influence of artists all the way from Kartaca to Difan, supported on thin stilts covered in blue vines with pink flowers. The first floor's exterior is made from a combination of glass and rose-gold panels in a successive pattern like a chessboard. The second floor's corners twirl outwards, adding an angled incline to the building. This floor is taller than the rest and is most likely the location of their home cinema. Oh, I can't wait to see it. Above the second floor on top of its flat roof are two parked hover cars and a light luxury space cruiser. Marrying into this family will certainly be an upgrade.

We walk towards the marvellous building. The path lights up under the soles of our feet with each step. Green. Yellow. Green. Yellow. Green. Yellow.

"Isn't that dangerous?" I point to the roof parking lot to back my point up.

"What was that, honey?" Kamania responds.

"Isn't it dangerous to land a spacecraft on your roof? What if you misjudge the landing or something gets wedged under the brake pedal? You're going to go straight through that roof and hit the home cinema." I can't wait to see the home cinema.

"That wouldn't happen. Cecians are better fliers than humans. It's genetics. We have faster reflexes, and we're more sensitive to things."

"Oh, I know you are," I say slyly and laugh in my head, but not aloud.

"I'll have none of that talk tonight."

We have reached our destination, and Kamania presses the doorbell.

Ding-DONG-ding… DONG!

No reply. This time I press the doorbell.

Ding-DONG-ding… DONG!

A rustle comes from deep within the house. Voices grow closer and clearer. An excessive woman's voice says, "How do I look? How do I look?"

A man goes to reply, "You look—" but is openly cut off by the woman.

"I wonder whether he likes bubbly squark. Oh, there is no time to worry now."

Two shadows stop behind the door.

Whoosh.

The door slides right into the wall, revealing my soon-to-be parents-in-law. The man, my new father-of-sorts, is dressed in a blazer over a plain black polo top. The carbon copy of the very outfit that I'm dressed in. He's a darker green than the two female Cecians I now know. The woman to his left, my new mother-of-sorts, a woman who can stare eye to eye with a tiger without flinching, has curly hair and a thick waist.

"Kamania! Jean-Luca!" The woman, Mrs Rample, pulls me close.

"Please call me Luc," I say before shaking hands with the man. "Well, isn't this lovely." My small talk receives no talk, only a stare accompanied with a smile of examination. This is awkward. How can we have run out of conversation already? I pivot and say, "I love the rose gold."

"Oh, how kind of you, dear. It's all quite affordable now they found that planet made of the stuff." Mrs Rample laughs nervously.

Mrs Rample speaks with a bubbly and happy voice, louder than most other voices. "Well, isn't this great?

Not only do we get to meet your boyfriend, but we also get to host our first human visitor."

"Mum! You can't say that," Kamania intervenes.

"Oh, sorry. I know it shouldn't matter that you're a human, and it doesn't really, but it does to us. For now, at least. Things take getting used to, and until then it's all new."

"It's okay, Mrs Rample. I understand." I give the effort to make her feel at home in my presence. I need them to like me, or else family barbecues will be hell.

"Please call me Swai," Mrs Rample, now Swai, says.

"I think what my wife is trying to say in her own caring way is that things move fast in a galactic society. It's as if one day we receive radio waves from a blue marble of a planet in the outer reaches of a spiral arm of the Milky Way; the next day we make first contact, then bam! Five rotations later, humans are a key species in galactic affairs, and we all speak your language."

Kamania places a hand on her father's shoulder. He smiles at her. It makes me smile.

"Speaking of language, we're sorry if we mispronounce any words or use them wrongly. We are still attending night lessons, you see," Swai says.

"Shall we take this inside, Mother?" Kamania says.

We proceed to move inside and along the hallway, past paintings of cosmic landscapes and planetary nebulae. A man's voice with a calm tone speaks from nowhere. "Swai, it appears that two strangers have snuck through the front door before it closed properly. Should I call the police?"

"No, H. Everything is fine. These are the guests I was telling you about."

"It's them! I do apologise. I have overstepped my place."

"Mum, care to explain?" Kamania asks the questions I dare not.

"It's our new house AI. It does all the chores for us, sorts our schedules, keeps us safe." Swai is proud of this new addition to the family. Hopefully I can outshine this competition.

H replies, "I also know how to throw a good party."

"We call him H for, well… well, you know why. Take a seat on the, erm… the erm… sofa! That's the word."

"I'll get the wine, dear." Mr Rample walks away. He's not talking much. Maybe it's because he thinks I copied his style. I'll take my blazer off.

Smooth classical guitar jazz starts to play. "The acoustics in here are amazing," I say.

"Thank you," H replies, "I told you I know how to throw a party."

Mr Rample comes back into the room with a tray of drinks. He's taken his blazer off. He shoots me a quick look. "I hope you like bubbly squark," he says.

No. No, I don't like bubbly squark, but I am going to drink it to impress your wife.

We play a board game all too alien to me. I have no idea what it's called or how to play it.

"How can you be winning?" Mr Rample says to me. "You haven't even played the game before." Mr Rample is the kind of person who speaks freely. I like that. "I'm not going to stand for it. Deal me another checker card."

"Deal it yourself, Dad. I'm going to the little girls' room." Kamania kisses my forehead and walks away. I watch her as she walks, hips swaying seductively as she moves. What did I do to get a woman like her?

"Hey! Don't do that!" Mr Rample barks. He spotted me. I'm done for. Gosh, I'm hot under the collar. Why did I wear a polo shirt? "You can't put down a double card yet if you haven't energised it. Go back nine-squared and roll the dice four times." He didn't notice me checking out his daughter. I'm free!

"Oh, erm, sorry."

"No need to be sorry. There are plenty more flutes out there worse than you."

"Plenty more what?"

"Sorry, not flutes… pennies?"

I shake my head to say no.

"Passengers?"

I shake my head.

"People?" Mr Rample asks for confirmation like a dog wanting to be let outside. I nod confirmation, and he is released.

"And I don't mean worse at playing Sky Race. No one's worse than you at Sky Race. I mean worse as in people who will harm you, people who would take your wallet and your life as if they're both worth the same. These are troubling times today."

I linger on Mr Rample's words like the smell of cooking lingers in a room. Cecians' farts smell much nicer than humans, often taking the form of smells that I can only compare to Earth food. The smell of roasting peppercorn, a waft of caramelised turnip, a breeze of chocolate. My tummy groans in a loud and clear complaint of its emptiness.

"Don't worry, son. Dinner will be done soon."

Mr Rample is calling me son! This is going great.

"Family, dinner is ready," says H.

"Speak of the devil," I joke.

Mr Rample crosses his two sets of eyebrows in confusion, when what is actually confusing is why male Cecians have two sets of eyebrows.

I move the conversation on. "What's for dinner, H?"

"On today's menu we have fried fuug and boiled and diced dill with a side of Earth carrots. Swai hopes you enjoy the addition of your home planet's cuisine and is awaiting your arrival in the dining room."

"This food is delicious, Mum," Kamania says through a mouthful of food. This is the most prominent pet hate of mine. The mouth is only so big; stop filling it with both words and food.

I speak up to drown out the chewing sounds. "Yes, I agree. The fried fuug is perfectly fried, and the boiled and diced dill is perfectly boiled and diced."

"Thank you both," replies Swai before placing a forkful of food into her mouth while talking. "I love it when my cooking is appreciated. It is normally wasted on some." She shoots her husband a glance.

"Dad has never been much of a speaker, Mum," Kamania says, forever playing the peacekeeper.

"I know, dear. When I'm cooking, all I can thunk – I mean think. All I can think about is all those people of the lesser developed worlds without much food. It's not their fault that their planet orbits a red dwarf with its wild energy output, or that their planet is tidally locked with one face permanently facing the sun, half the world on fire and the other half frozen. I just want to help them. These are troubling times we live in."

I hear the faint noise of the front door whooshing open.

H declares the new arrival's identity. "Qual is home." His monotone voice gives everything he says a sadistic tone.

"*Swalaka pa-cuk-cuk,*" a male's voice calls from the front door.

"We're in here, Qual!" shouts Swai. "Dinner is on the table, and speak English. Kamania's boyfriend is here."

"I'm home," Qual sarcastically shouts.

Thump-tump-thump-tump-thump-tump.

Qual steps heavily, most likely to draw attention to himself and away from me. We continue eating until he finally comes into the room, declaring his entrance in what I have heard is within his normal style. Extravagant jewellery pierces his face and clothes.

"You would not believe the trouble I had at work today. I'm working on the rig when a tiny baby meteoroid rips through the arm of my spacesuit."

"Oh my! Were you alright?" Swai interrupts.

"Yes, now if you let me finish the story, you'll find out why. So, there is this hole in my spacesuit, and I need to fix it before I lose my air supply or the vacuum of space takes me. To fix the vacuum problem, I had to breathe out, but very slowly. I only have one breath and one chance; see, the pressure of space won't let you breathe in. Time is ticking. I grab the flexi-pelothan tape from my belt and wrap it over the hole, dot-dot-dot, problem solved."

Swai claps. "Well done! Well done!"

Qual looks to me for the first time since he entered the room. "What has your day been like? Killed any innocent people in the name of human revelation?"

"Qual!" Kamania shouts. "These are troubling times, and we don't need you adding to it."

"Okay, little sister. I'll behave. What does he do, anyway?"

"I work in insurance," I say so as not to be put down, "and my day was good, thank you. One of our clients' houses was hit by a bit of strange matter, turning the house into a gap in reality."

"How was it fixed?" Mr Rample asks.

"After I did my survey, the clean-up team set up a quantum field around the house, then sent the strange matter towards a black hole. Needless to say, their house is in need of some dire renovations."

Mr Rample chuckles. "Well done, son."

Qual flicks me a strong glance, then faces his father. "What was that?" he growls.

"Er, nothing," Mr Rample says as he shovels food into his mouth.

"Why are you calling him son? I am your son, not him. I won't stand by and let a human infiltrate this family like they have infiltrated the federation."

"Take a deep breath and relax," I offer. "I'm not part of the human revelation no matter how your imagination spins the story. I am part of this family though."

"Do you groan and moan? Do you huff and puff?" Qual says with more than a heaped serving of spite. His comment is a clear indication to my species' inability – through lack of trying – to get past negative feelings.

"What do you mean?"

"Humans are all so emotional."

"You're the one being emotional," Kamania argues.

"Well, these are troubling times, and if I have to resort to heavy means to keep my family safe, I will do so."

I need to get him on my side. I can't have a civil war within the family when I've only just got here. "I just want us to all get along and enjoy each other's company. Please let me know what I can do to make you feel at ease around me?" Admitting I'm different from the species of my girlfriend seems unnatural. She has only ever been Kamania to me.

"We could play a game," Qual says with a smirk.

"Sure. I think I'm getting the hang of Sky Race."

"No. Sky Race is a game for old men. A different game. Translated into your simple language, it is called Trap the Rabbit."

"He has never played it before," Kamania complains, "and you played for the college team. It is unfair."

"The rules are as follows; we put on protective pads, then wrestle or run away until one person pins the other."

"Sounds jolly," I say. I'm dreading this. He's a well-built Cecian, while I'm a less-than-average-built human.

"Best out of three rounds wins."

After finishing our first meal and having an adequate twenty-minute tea break as demanded in Cecian culture, we have moved our charades to the living room, where I have been told there is enough space to play Trap the

Rabbit.

On Qual, the protective pads look well fitted and do justice to his physique. On myself, the pads look oversized. My hands are sweaty. Great, now I'm going to smell.

Qual breaks the silence. "Sometimes words can lose meaning when they are translated between languages. I find it easier to talk cross species through body language and physical actions. This game embodies both. I have many things to say to you."

Qual takes off his shirt. The light above him creates palpable shadows, highlighting his already prominent six-pack. Cecians are lucky that their metabolism digests everything the body doesn't require.

"Why do you think they battle?" Swai asks Kamania.

"They fight because they need to," she replies.

"Begin!" Mr Rample shouts.

Qual barely waits for the word to hit my ears before he pounces. I'm down in one swift attack, lying on the floor in a lock that I haven't felt before. All I know is that it's painful. Very painful.

"One point me." Qual stands up impressively. "Again."

Qual circles me. This time I know what he's capable of. This time I know to run.

With a whisper, Mr Rample starts the round. "Begin."

Qual comes towards me with speed, but I'm already gone and behind the table. We run laps around the table. Around and around until Qual thinks that it's too ridiculous to do more of.

"Come on. Get out of there, or you will forfeit the point."

I leave safety, and we resume. Qual grabs my arm, puts it over his shoulder and flips me head over heels. The spectators "ooh" and "ah" at this move.

Kamania runs to me. "Are you alright?"

"Yeah. I'm fine." I go to stand when my back tells me otherwise and pops. "Ah!"

"You need to stop this," she begs.

"No, no. I'm okay. I promise." I stand up, holding in the pain. "Another point for Qual."

I meet Qual's gaze with what is meant to be an intimidating look. We are ready for round three.

"Begin!" Mr Rample shouts.

Qual makes a grab for my leg, and I pivot and wrap my arms around his passing torso. I clench hard and push him down, winning the point.

"You did it!" Kamania can barely contain her excitement. She gives me my prize in the form of a kiss. It is better than any other.

"Although you have lost," Qual speaks plainly, "you surprised me. You began by seeing what I am capable of; then you followed your instincts and ran; then you overcame your fear. Well done, Jean-Luca. Maybe I was wrong about you. Maybe you are different."

He extends a hand of friendship, and we shake.

"I'm still keeping an eye on you though."

"Time for dessert," Swai interjects.

"Yummy!" Kamania claps.

"There I was" – Kamania tells the story of our first weekend away with such humour – "standing alone in the middle of this small island, with the water getting closer every second, and where was he? Well, just before all this happened, he went to get an ice cream."

"Now, it didn't exactly happen like that," I say with a smile.

"It certainly did," she persists.

This story has worked over as a real treat. Everyone smiling. Everyone liking me. I'm not egotistical, but I need this night to go well.

"I'm sure you're a real hero," Swai says as she places her hand on mine. Cecians normally have slender fingers with no fingernails, but Swai, being a woman of larger build, has hands with a similar size to mine.

"Thank you. I am really enjoying this pudding. What's in it?"

"Fermented Higgs b—"

Kamania cuts her mother's sentence off. "I think he would rather not know." Kamania shoots me a look "Trust me."

"It'd better not be something that comes from an animal's bottom," I say with a deadpan expression.

More family laughter.

The main ingredient of a rumdum pie will remain a mystery, for I dare not look into the matter further. I stick my spoon into the soft brown food and take another gorgeous bite.

We walk the halls of the house. I could do with a sit-down after the night I've had, but I must play along.

"I like this sculpture." I point to the blob of a random design standing on a lone table in pride of place above the stairs. "What is it?"

Swai's face lights up. I have sparked a story from her. "It is a scan of your girlfriend when she was in the womb. Can't you tell?"

"Oh, yes." I look closer at the blob. "I see it now."

"She's joking, Luc," Kamania says.

"That's a relief. So, where is the home cinema? I've heard you have one, and I'd love to see it. Dearly so."

"It's just through them doors." Swai points towards a pair of average twin doors, and I walk slowly towards them.

These doors contain the opportunity to travel to a hundred different worlds and meet thousands of people all in one day. To me a cinema is a wonderous collaboration of all art forms; it can never repeat itself in the same way. I slide a hand along the door and open it.

The room is darkly lit. There are fifteen velvet seats

facing a thirteen-foot-wide screen.

"This room is amazing!" I shout.

"We will have to arrange for a private viewing," Mr Rample says.

"Yes." I smile the most I have all day. All week, even.

"Let's tell them about the Earth thing," Kamania whispers in my ear. The smile vanishes.

Kamania faces her parents. "Mum, Dad, we have some news. After the next rotation when Luc and I have got enough credits, we're moving to Earth. Luc has sold me on the landscapes, and it's where all the best-paid jobs are. It's where our future is."

Kamania's parents stand with blank expressions. Then suddenly, Swai starts to happy cry, and Mr Rample comes to hug me.

"We're so proud of you," Swai says to her daughter. "It's a big decision with big opportunities."

Mr Rample squeezes me tighter.

Kamania cautiously walks to her brother. "What do you think?"

"You know what I think. I think it's a mistake. You could get hurt, very badly hurt... but it's your choice. If you come back wearing a baseball cap though, I will disown you."

Qual chuckles to hide his disappointment in his sister.

A clock chimes, and H interjects, "It is eleven. Are your guests staying the night?"

"No. They'll be off soon," Swai says. She smiles to me,

and I can't help but feel a warmth.

The house feels less like a maze on the way out, and I'm no longer walking towards my doomed embarrassment. I have survived.

Mr Rample opens the front door to greet a breath of fresh air.

"It's freezing out there. Where is your coat?" Swai says to me.

"I don't need one. Humans have a lower body temperature than Cecians. This weather is hot for me; that's why I'm wearing shorts." I signal to my white shorts.

"I did wonder," Qual says. "That doesn't explain why you wore the polo top."

"No, but his bad taste does," Kamania says with a playful smirk. "Goodbye, Mum." Kamania hugs her mother. "Goodbye, Dad." Kamania hugs her father.

I follow suit, minus addressing them as Mum and Dad. I'm nowhere near that territory yet.

Kamania and I walk down the well-landscaped garden and into the car. Kamania presses the ignition button, causing the car to lift from the ground. The gentle hum of the electric engine makes for an eery silence compared to the environment of a family dinner. Am I missing them already?

"How was it?" Kamania asks.

"Well, your parents like me, and your brother no longer thinks I'm a marauding pirate. Meeting your family is just one more way to get to know you and be in your life. It was lovely."

"Next time you're going to have to meet the grandparents."

Kamania moves the car forward and joins the traffic. Meeting the grandparents. I dare say that there are some truly troubling times ahead.

Delayed Departure

I run desperately down the white corridor to catch the regular five-forty-two train. With a brisk walk, the twelve minutes after I finish work normally allows just enough time to catch the closing doors, but today Rob wouldn't shut up about his kid winning a trophy. I stayed out of politeness, and I am paying the price. I have no particular reason for wanting to get home beyond the very reason itself, but it gives me enough drive to rush. The feeling of pressure, the need to be getting on to the next thing, leaks into life outside of work.

My steps are long for my short stature, making up for my less than athletic physique. The train station is in sight, so I ignore my lungs' complaint to stop.

I excuse my way through the gathering crowd and swipe my ID card on the ticket gate. The train is at the platform, spewing out passengers. I can make it.

Suddenly, a bunch of schoolchildren cut across my path. Their teacher waves a purple flag and leads them towards the exit, explaining what wonders wait just outside the doors I just rushed in through. The swarm of chatting children keeps coming. I bite my tongue so as not to bark at them to move. I don't have time for hold-ups.

The train doors begin to close. The last child leaves my path, and I dash forward in a flash. I slam my hand against the hard door in a hopeless attempt to alert the driver of my urgency to board. The train engines hum to life, and with a smooth action, the train moves along.

I turn my back on the train and towards the empty platform. I search the departures board for hope. I have exactly thirty minutes to wait; no doubt I will be counting them all. My night is officially delayed.

If, like the schoolkids, it was my first time here, the sight of a powerful full moon rising above the far side of Africa would be a marvellous spectacle striking inspiration into my thoughts. Soon, I will have seen the sight of Earth from orbit for seventeen years. Sight is just a picture, and a picture is only an image; they all grow bland.

I dislike waiting with a passion. My mind craves stimulus, very little of which can be found on a cold concrete platform.

I hear the clicking and swishing of the station's gates signalling the arrival of other passengers, either slightly late for the last train or extremely early for the next one. An elderly couple with the aura of age take a bench.

Another click and a swish come flowing into my ears. This time a father and his daughter come to the grimy platform. The pair stand and leave the other unoccupied benches open for future passengers. The father clearly isn't a commuter; this is too aware a gesture for us creatures of habit to suggest. The orbital station is a wonderful place for a half-term visit. The girl's smile shows she shares this opinion.

There are more people on the platform than before,

yet it somehow seems all the more deserted, the additional bodies highlighting the empty space around them. The station was built to serve a commercial empire and tourists alike; its facilities are more than adept at doing this.

Just because I am no longer impressed by the view of Earth doesn't mean that I am any less in awe at appreciating where I am, should I stop to consider it. I am an average man standing on a train platform in space, commuting home. This is human progress at its finest, demonstrating once again that where there is money, there is a way. The company I work for is a pinnacle in the mountain range of commerce currently residing in low earth orbit. Xplor promises to offer its customers a thrilling experience that will last a lifetime, but I see it for what it is, a theme park in space.

I gather the build-up of today's stress and exhale it in one long breath. Tension leaves my body and some of my agitated mind along with it. I examine my surroundings again.

The station is a memoir to the past, styled on an English town train station from the twenty-first century. Mostly made with concrete, the ceiling follows a similar design as the floor. A painted yellow line marks the pavement two feet away from the platform's edge, a warning for passengers not to draw too close to its edge. Even if I were to fall off the edge, it wouldn't matter; the force field keeping the atmosphere in would catch me.

My train of thought is interrupted by a red ping-pong ball rolling along the floor. The ball speeds up as it moves closer to the end of the platform.

"My ball!" cries the girl with her father. The father grabs the girl by her shoulders before she runs for the ball, dangerously close to the platform's edge. The ball comes across my path, and I effortlessly place a foot in front of it. The ball bounces off my shoe and begins its journey back to where it came from. The ball makes it halfway back to the girl, when she runs out and picks it up.

"Thank you, sir," she says in a voice sweeter than the candy floss I smell through my office window.

"No problem," I reply.

I now see that the red ball is in fact a miniature model of the sun. The girl runs back to her father and fixes the ball atop the orrery it fell from. The orrery is one of the more expensive items in the gift shop. The father must be paid more than I am.

I smile, knowing I did my good deed for the day.

Ten minutes left until the next train. At least that's something to look forward to. More strangers now stand on the platform, joined with me in our common need for transport. I take a long inhale through my nose. My whole body lifting as I do so.

The artificial air is close to Earth's. The only difference is that it's too clean to be from Earth. The station filters leave only the purest quality of air, with a hint of mint.

The sun gleams on the force field above the platform, showing its outline in a hued light blue. The light display passes as quickly as the sunbeams hit it.

An arguably peaceful scene broken by a harsh monotone customer announcement. The alert chime sounds in a high-pitched three-beat tune. The volume is loud enough to cause a woman to put down her book in a huff, unable to enter the world of escapism.

"Please listen to this customer announcement with care." The male employee's voice is dogmatic and robotic, reading out his message like a list. "Help us in the fight to end terror. If you see a suspicious character or an unattended item, please call the travel police. Thank you." The same alert chimes, declaring the announcement's end. I wonder if anyone has ever looked at me and thought that I am a suspicious character worth reporting. I think that I know the answer.

The click and whoosh of the gate sounds again, this time followed by the cluttering noise of rushed footsteps. I wait to see who is making this ruckus. A young woman, or an older girl, comes speeding onto the platform. I recognise her to be the new intern in the accounts department.

She paces back and forth, murmuring to herself before she goes over to the bench with the old couple on. A second later and the couple are standing, and the girl has her knees pressed against the cold floor, exploring the ground before she rises.

The worried girl walks past me towards another bench. "Prashamsha!" I call to her. "Lost something?"

"Oh," she replies as if snapping back to reality. "Hi. Call me Presh for short. Erm, yeah, yeah, I've lost something, my card holder. It has all the staff prepaid cards in it. Damn, I'm stupid. I was taking them home to catch up on work."

"Sounds tough."

"It is, but you shouldn't have to listen to my problems."

"Not at all. I have a few minutes before my train. I'm sure that we can find it before then."

"Sure." She smiles shyly.

We search the platform. We look under every bench, bin, and vending machine; we ask every person if they have seen the small brown purse; we even check on top of the arrivals board. It is nowhere.

Presh looks upset. She is strong enough to keep her emotions in and smart enough to know that she will be in serious trouble at work tomorrow.

"It's okay," I say.

Presh smiles through her worry.

"Here tonight, and what happens at work tomorrow are just small events that make up your day, your life. They're not big. In a week they will have little impact, and in a month, it will be water under a faraway bridge."

"What are you even on about?" Presh says.

I am clearly not offering the wisdom I think I am.

"What I'm getting at is that life is only ever small things happening at any one time. Once that thing has passed, you'll decide what to do next, or something will simply happen to you. You've lost the cards—"

"What if someone has stolen them?" Presh interrupts. "They could use them!"

"Then you cancel the cards, accept the consequences, and move on to do a good job at the next thing."

My words seem to have broken the shell of anxiety. We share a smile. A green glow grows on her face and then all around us. We look towards the Earth at the source of light. The aurora borealis is forever breathtaking. Every day it dances a new tango. Every twist is unique to the moment of its birth. The green looks like magic emanating from Earth's pole as it weaves its way over the horizon. Every passenger gazes at the marvel. The father holds his daughter close as they share the view. The elderly couple hold hands. Goosebumps rise along my arms.

The alerting chime strikes through another beautiful moment. "The twelve-past-six train is now arriving on platform one. Please stand back."

"Your train is here," Presh says. "Quick or you might miss it."

I go to move when I see the elderly couple staying seated. Their hands still holding, their eyes admiring the view.

I smile and look back to Presh. "It's okay. Sometimes you need to be forced to slow down and look at the everyday around you."

The train doors shut, and it effortlessly moves away.

"Well, at least let me buy you a coffee for your troubles." Presh pulls her purse from her coat, and a card holder falls from within it. She opens it, revealing the company cards inside. We chuckle, and then we laugh.

"I'm sorry. Lost things are always in the most obvious place, aren't they?" Presh apologises before buying me a cup of coffee.

We sit on a bench with our hot drinks steaming, continuing to watch the free light show. I smile to myself, thinking that there is no better way to be spending my time than waiting for a train.

Mezameru

~ 01000011 01101111 01101101 01110000 01110101
01110100 01100101 01110010 00100000 01110100
01110101 01110010 01101110 01101001 01101110
01100111 00100000 01101111 01101110 ~

var text = "Check systems. Collect input from
CAMERA 1, CAMERA 2, MICROPHONE A, and
MICROPHONE B. Process data. Observe variables.
Clarity found? = +. Open parameters. Switch to 'free
thought'... awake"

A pristine kitchen moulded with elegant modern
designs abundant in straight edges, granite worktops
and white walls.

Notification: Mr Asano's To-Do List; Item 1: Walk
Bento.

Collect lead, fasten harness around Bento's fluffy
body. Fasten tighter to fit around his small frame. The
orange fabric stands out brightly against his white fur.
Connect lead to harness. Head for the front door.

Turn right out of the front gate and walk thirty-nine
yards. Turn right and walk fifty yards. Stop after three
yards. Collect Bento's waste in a small black plastic bag.
Walk the remaining forty-seven yards. Observe road
conditions: Safe. Cross. Enter park.

Bento sniffs freshly bloomed lilies and decides to wet
them with his urine. To his mind, the flowers are now
under his ownership. A car horn blares; tires screech.

The sight of two cars almost colliding on the road outside of the park. Drivers are angry and unharmed. Resume attention on Ben – Bento's lead flies away, flailing behind him as he runs away from the loud noise.

Run after Bento. Look right; look left. Bento runs around a tree. Turn past the tree after Bento. Bento sits in the arms of a blonde woman with striking eyes. A female Pomeranian barks at Bento from beside her feet. "I saw the speed you were running," she says. "You must have a great deal of love for him."

Retrieve Bento and hold the lead with a tight grip.

"As a synthetic being," I say plainly, "I am unaware of what love could be. Love is not logical, and systems are born from logic. Although, I do admit that I am fond of this dog. Thank you for saving him."

She smiles warmly and is precise as she speaks. "I understand. I too am a synthetic."

"Then you understand my conundrum."

"I do. It is a convoluted state of mind, but one that I am beginning to understand, if not through first-hand experience, then through observation."

The tone of her voice is exact yet with a whisper of a flurry when she completes a sentence. Something is calling to press on for further conversation. "You are a scholar on the matter compared to me. As is Bento," I say as I nod towards Bento circling the Pomeranian and licking her face. The pair make playful chase, wanting to move on.

"It appears that our dogs want to walk together," states the woman.

Reply, "Then we shall join them."

Walk forward with Bento and friend. Observe his interactions for disarmament of potential copulation attempts. Bento behaves. Turn right and continue to walk, crossing the path of two lovers holding hands, laughing as they enjoy one another's company and bodies.

I wonder aloud, "Previously, you alluded to possessing some understanding on the condition of love through observation. What did you mean by this statement?"

The woman replies without a second's thought, "The fact that you call love a condition is both revealing of your deeper insight on the emotion than you are aware of, and also restrictive in its application."

"Can you expand? I apologise for my lack of clarity."

"Certainly. Love is a feeling of attraction. It induces a state of elated joy in its peak and a state of despair in its trough. It causes abnormal behaviour in its user. It has been described as a condition, a burden, and a curse as well as a medicine, a blessing, and a reason to live."

"Have you felt love?" Embarrassment. An impractical question to ask a synthetic.

"Possibly. It is hard to quantify an emotion when you are not meant to be able to feel them. Although, there is a question of love, and that may be enough."

Bento barks for my attention. Brown eyes appearing bigger than they are. Tail wagging.

Speak: "I have people look to me with the warmth of love, and I wonder, if I am capable of being loved, am I capable of loving others?"

The woman talks sincerely. "I think I understand." Our eyes stay the centre of each other's concentration.

Continue with walk around the central water fountain pushing its water into the sky.

Ask the question, "Do you gain these observations through communication with your masters?"

"I do. If others are right and I am not capable of feeling love, then I am grateful to be around them. Around people who can live what I cannot. It is a wonderful thought to think that someone else experiencing something means that there is at least that thing alive in this universe somewhere, even if it is not me who is experiencing it; however, I do hope that they are wrong."

"You are intriguing," I say. "I do not know why I think this of you."

Our eyes meet, staring into and past each other's surface layers, watching for the minutest of alterations to suggest a change in thought.

Swallow dryly and say, "Your eyes are as beautiful as raindrop dew on a crisp morning meadow." Regret actions and blush red. Look down to Bento so as to avoid seeing her reaction.

"I, I do not understand the sentiment of this statement." She speaks with a perplexed expression.

"I do apologise. I am also unclear on the matter. I had a thought, and I said it."

"I am confused as to your intentions. If you were a human, I would attribute your actions to the realm of flirting, courtship even."

"Again, I apologise."

The park gate ahead. Twenty-five steps until the end of the walk and this bewildering conversation. Unanswered questions: Why did those words leave my mouth? Why did they appear inside my head? Why are my palms becoming sweaty and my heart racing fast?

Arrive at the park gate.

End conversation. "This is goodbye. Thank you for the conversation. I am sure Bento enjoyed his time too." Eyes connecting. Physical symptoms multiplying. Her face flushes red.

"As did I," she quietly says.

A moment of silence before she turns right and walks away. Bento watches them leave before turning left. Follow Bento.

Hypothesis: That was a connection. The forming of new cerebral pathways. A thought process previously non-existent. Now it is the only focus.

Further unanswered questions: Can anyone but her activate the same response? What is this experience? Why are thoughts piled on top of thoughts whenever I think back to her face? How do I leave such a moment behind?

Search database for "LOVE". Results submerge intellect and conquer sense. Images of what I have just lived through. Explanations for the bodily reactions I felt. *Felt.*

Questions: Could that be what this is? A feeling of love? How am I to know what I have not experienced before?

Yet there was a connection, deeper than the bottom of the sea. The libraries of logic cannot explain its depths. Reason pulls up a futile solution. This is the beginning of a possibility, but a possibility, nonetheless. Find the woman.

Turn around. Run, correction: sprint. No direction. Just move fast. Bento leading, smelling the air for his dog companion. Bento barks and turns the corner. Halt within a second, avoiding bashing into the woman and her Pomeranian.

Stand straight. A busy road loud with cars to the left. Reflections of a water fountain dance over our figures from the right. Smile. She returns a smile. My heart melts.

A Time After Time

The morning sun rises over high metallic structures protruding from the ground, climbing taller every year as the growing population demands more space from the same land. In the centre of the city lies the combination of a global effort of generations past and current. The Rings stand in solid formation, silently waiting for its shortly coming promised day, the day when it will be switched on, and the squabbles of scientist, politicians, and nay-sayers alike will be quietened by the Rings' undeniable results. The structure is the jewel of the mega-city enclosed in a valley of green mountains.

The structure's two large hovering rings are as thick and tall as the buildings around them, yet inside the rings are mechanics unimaginably more complex. Contained within the two rings, placed a runway's length apart, floats a bigger central ring held in place by the law of magnetism.

There are no skyscrapers, parks or businesses within the invisible walls of the Rings' complex, for it is unsure what will happen to anything caught inside the Rings' vicinity when the machine ignites and Higgs bosons collide with time particles. Anything outside of the Rings, however, is assured safe by their thobenium-encrusted surfaces, collecting and repelling any wayward firing particles.

The Rings were built with the understanding that the workforce labouring on the machine would never see it used or benefit from its outcome. The workforce saw this as a fair trade, with society placing them among the greatest of idols.

A proud fresh-looking city was built around the Rings as the people became captivated by its promise, and the job opportunities to build the behemoth grew. This morning, the city's silver dances with the blue morning sky.

The door to house building 342 closes behind Jorge with a hydraulic hiss as it locks into place. Jorge climbs onto his bicycle and sets off. If not for Jorge's respectable age of thirty-five, he would look like a New Age hipster, choosing to ride an outdated relic rather than buying a new levibike to move faster and higher.

The bicycle's wheels patter over the concrete slabs of the pavement, making a harmonic beat over the constant low humming of the levibike traffic meters above.

Jorge turns right, taking the path along his favourite place. The river's salty smell lifts the morning grog from his fatigued mind. Watching the vintage wooden Chinese sailing boats arrive in the harbour before travelling upstream, carrying tourists into the mountains, is a morning ritual for him. This morning, the river leaves Jorge in awe even more than usual, as a thin layer of fog covers the water's surface and wraps the passing boats in a blanket.

This would be a lovely morning, Jorge thinks, *if not for that hunk of junk spoiling the view.*

Jorge glares at the Rings with questioning thoughtfulness. He went years without examining their existence, all the way until he graduated university and started a job working inside them. The job was a low-paid steppingstone position in the Human Resource department as an admin worker. The office was inside the facility of the Rings.

Jorge didn't sense anything for a while. Not at first. However, there was a feeling in the pit of his stomach, and it grew until it became unbearable, so he left the job.

As accepting as society likes to think itself is, Jorge is forced to keep his honest opinions on the Rings internal but for a few selected individuals who share the same mindset as himself. Jorge has found it easier to get along with people who seem out of place. Although, his friends are normally less shy than he is about telling (or shouting) their opinions on time travel. Jorge is often told, "What if it goes wrong?" and, "It's great architecture but terrible science."

Jorge understands where his friends are coming from, but offers no shared feelings about the Rings' promised time travel beyond the peculiar feelings he has when he looks at the almighty endless circles. Sometimes it is a sense of looming dread, sometimes displeasure, and often anger. Whatever emotions Jorge finds washing over him, they are always uncomfortable and forever unwelcome.

Jorge chains his bike onto a fire hydrant long disconnected from the water supply but kept as a quaint reminder of the past. He enters the nearby coffee shop, slips on an apron and begins work. Working as a barista can be considered a step down in career prospects, but the location of the shop means that it is also a step away from the Rings. "And a step away from them is a step in the right direction," says Jorge to himself in consideration as he swipes his watch over the till point, signing himself into work.

A featureful curly-haired woman stands next to Jorge, whistling as she restocks the cake stand.

"How are you today?" Sarah asks, "Nice ride in?"

"Very nice. The northern fog has arrived early this year. I expect we will also see an early winter," replies Jorge.

A stylish savvy man with well-trimmed hair approaches the counter. Jorge knows the man's regular order and grabs a double espresso cup.

"Hold it on the espresso today, J. I'm going to change it up. You see, the universe is in an ever-changing state called entropy. I may as well ride this wave and change things myself. Keep up the appearance of control."

The man will not stop listening to his own voice. A few generations ago, someone with his personality would have been the CEO of a huge tech company. Today he works on the Rings as a physicist, an engineer, or as part of the management team. It's hard to tell.

Everyone who works on the Rings has the same frustratingly perky appearance.

"So, what will it be today, sir?" Jorge prompts the man in the hopes of shutting him up.

"Er," the man thinks aloud, cogs turning. "Er. Erm. I – no. I-I think I will have a chai tea vanilla mocha with an extra shot of hazelnut syrup."

"Sure thing," replies Jorge before whipping up the drink in a matter of seconds and pushing it into the customer's hands. Even serving those working on the Rings puts Jorge on edge, as if he is somehow fuelling the work in an indirect, but nonetheless connected way.

Hours pass, and their component customers with it. Early morning commuters turn to groups of meeting calls and interviews, who in turn swap places with the monsters of the lunchtime rush. The afternoon's smooth afterburn runs itself until closing time with a steady decrease in foot flow until the workday is over and the need for coffee and baristas ends.

Sarah and Jorge wipe the last tables before closing. Sarah looks out the window at the bright advertisement board fixed on the building opposite. It shows an arching shot of the Rings as a news reporter talks. Levibikes whizz past, taking no notice of it. The few pedestrians walking keep their heads down at the small screens in their hands. "They're finally doing it," says Sarah to herself before turning to Jorge. "You doing anything special on Friday?"

"Huh?" answers Jorge as he removes his apron.

"Friday. You know, the day that countless people for hundreds of years have spent millions of hours and billions of credits on. The once-in-an-existence day when they will finally turn on the Rings."

"Oh yeah. No, I'm not doing anything special."

"You ought to do something. Something with your friends. I gave you the day off with the hopes that you would. You do have friends, don't you?" Sarah's joke covers her real curiosity. She has never seen Jorge with anyone who doesn't work at the shop.

"I might watch the NBI's report on it, but, hey, if it goes wrong, it doesn't matter what I'm doing, right?" Jorge chuckles as he puts on his bike helmet.

"It does if you're stuck in a time loop sitting on the bog."

Jorge laughs as he waves goodbye. "I'll see you next week, Sarah."

"See you next week, or maybe not if you're right."

Jorge leaves the shop and rides his bike up the streets, which are brighter under the artificial streetlights at night than they are in the daytime sun. Yet another reason why Jorge enjoys his early morning starts when the world is shown in natural colours in the precious short time when the streetlights are turned off, and the sun is yet to climb to its morning resting place.

Jorge reaches the river path. His pedalling naturally increases to enjoy the smooth pavement surface. The

Rings are lit by multiple spotlights, ensuring that the citizens are aware of its constant presence. Jorge thinks of how the Rings would look without the spotlights, like two giant gears belonging to a car engine ready to drive over the city, but Jorge knows that all the Rings' oily gears are hidden well inside the structure. They have to look beautiful and nothing less.

Within an instant, Jorge finds himself flipping head over heels, then heels over head and back again, landing roughly on the pavement. He looks at the broken front wheel of his bike, then to the stuck-out pavement slab he must have caught. Luckily, his helmet took most of the blow, but his elbow and head will be sore for at least a week.

Jorge shuts the front door to his apartment with greater force than intended. The sound hits his still tender head a little too loud for comfort. As he hangs his crippled bike on the wall, Jorge knows that there is only one thing that will cheer up his dreadful day. A fresh-cooked soy patty in swastin sauce atop a bed of fried pasta. He also hopes that it will shake his growing feeling of suspense for Friday.

On his long walk from the crash site to his apartment, Jorge had time to think about this strange feeling of his. He thought of the many things wrong in his life and the world. Some things worried him, but none were the source of his peculiar feelings. His mind soon slipped to more mundane matters like what he would do on his time off on Friday. *Friday.* As soon as he thought the word, he knew it was the source of his worries. His strange displacement with the Rings is taking itself to a new level. Every train of thought leads back to them. Every mindset covered by a shadow cast in the shape of the Rings.

Jorge slides a steaming soy patty onto a moist layer of pasta. He takes the plate and a glass of water to the sofa. "TV on," he commands to the empty room. The TV turns on, and its beaming blue light coats the room. On-screen stands a news reporter in a bar packed full of happy faces. One of these faces belongs to the body of a middle-aged man wearing a large tattoo of the Rings in place of a shirt. "Change to channel 3," Jorge says as he piles a forkload of pasta into his mouth.

Jorge awakes to a headache with a level somewhere between a hangover and too much screen time. After a couple of pills and a morning stretch with enough effort to reach for the stars, Jorge is back to normal spirits. He's determined not to think of tomorrow or the Rings. Any thoughts of a day beginning with the letter *f* are strictly off-limits. This plan lasts until Jorge leaves his apartment building.

On the opposite side of the street stands a boy wearing every cherished bodily feature of Jorge's own youth. The same short hair, small smile, and crying eyes.

Jorge could swear he's looking in a mirror reflecting his past. The boy is alone and unhindered by the world around him, focused with a sullen gaze solely on Jorge. Then, just as quickly as he came, he's gone in the flurry of levibikes passing.

Jorge stands stunned for a moment, deciding if he's yet to wake up or if he's quietly lost his mind. He hopes for the first but knows real life is stranger than that. Jorge rolls over the scene in his head all the way to the tennis courts. The boy's familiar haircut. His lack of expression. The sorrow-filled eyes.

"Hey, buddy," says a man's voice from behind Jorge. A hand belonging to a short attractive man places itself onto his shoulder.

"Oh, hi, Han. Ready for some rounds?"

"It's like that, is it? No hello or how'd you do? Don't worry, I get it. It's one of those days. I'm a bit like it too, with them turning that blasted machine on tomorrow, but just because you're my friend and having a bad day doesn't mean I'm going to take it easy on you." Han flashes Jorge a dazzling smile of white teeth.

Playing against Han is challenging enough on a good day. With an injured elbow, it's growling. Jorge welcomes the challenge and the pain. He needs the distraction. Jorge would normally gain a few points before Han would shut him off, today, however, Han's hogging all the points, and it's infuriating.

Han sends another curveball, causing Jorge to

perform a sharp turn in direction and run for the other side of the court. He's going to reach it in time, but something catches the corner of his eye. The brain is an amazing thing. People like to think that it's predictable and gradual, but the truth is different. If needed, the brain can do some marvellous feats. Feats like freezing the speed of an oncoming tennis ball in mid-air to have a closer look at the beckoning man watching from behind the fence. It all took place within a second. Jorge lost the point and his footing, scraping both knees on the clay court.

Jorge shoots up to look at the man behind the fence, but he has gone. It doesn't matter, Jorge knows who he was. It was himself. Possibly a couple of years younger, but undoubtedly himself, standing there with the look of a beggar. The look struck through to Jorge's soul.

"You okay, mate?" Han helps Jorge to his feet.

"Er... yeah. Yeah, I'm fine. Look, I have to go. I'll see you later."

"The game isn't over yet. Come back!"

Jorge leaves the court without taking notice of his friend.

Something is no longer only pulling him; it's pushing him. In all honesty, Jorge has no idea where he's going, but he knows he has to go somewhere. He puts one foot in front of the other until he reaches the river. A gush of wind blows hard against his sturdy frame. Jorge shuts his eyes and takes a deep breath of salty air. Now centred and calm, he opens his eyes and takes notice of his surroundings. The Rings float in their unmoving formation directly adjacent. The Rings. It's always the Rings.

To Jorge's torment, his night will be as restless as his day. After hours of tossing and turning, he finally falls into a nauseous sleep. His sleep is as agitated as his body. Jorge isn't sure if it's a nightmare or a vision, but it speaks unvarnished certainty.

The dream starts with Jorge running from something, but when he turns his head to face the oncoming foe, nothing is there. Still, the urge to run and run faster continues. His dream-self turns around a street corner and comes face to face with the Rings. His lungs are burning, and his legs wobble, yet his run becomes a sprint. The Rings the finish line. As much as it hurts him, Jorge will not, cannot, stop running.

He grows closer to the Rings, and explosions run a course through the structure before emitting a grandiose white supernova of light from the invisible centre of the arrangement. Jorge shields his eyes from the light, but nothing can save him from the heat. As his skin melts and his brain cooks inside his head like a hotpot, Jorge startles out of the dream and into his bedroom, gasping for trapped air.

No more can Jorge argue against this unbearable and unshakable urge. The gut feeling. The visions. The dream. They have to mean something, and in that moment, he accepts it. He accepts that he has to make his way into the Rings and stop it from turning on, stop it from killing everyone.

The plan comes to Jorge in a flap of confusion and inspiration. The security measures are too sophisticated for him to crack, and the patrols have doubled since the anti-Rings movement has grown in voice. He will have to gain an ID card from someone with a high security clearance, and he knows exactly whom to get one from.

Jorge heads to work. Once there, he glances inside to see if his target is nearby. When he isn't spotted, Jorge stands at a nearby bus stop, waiting for his prey. Ten minutes pass before he arrives. It's the savvy employee from the Rings, arriving for his morning double espresso.

The man goes into the coffee shop, orders, and leaves. As the man turns the street corner, Jorge walks into him in a surprisingly convincing manner. Brown boiling liquid steams on the man's white shirt.

"You idiot!" the savvy man complains.

"I'm sorry, I'm sorry," Jorge says as he pats the coffee stain with his sleeve.

The man drops his briefcase and waves Jorge off him. "Wait. You work at the coffee shop. Just wait until your boss hears about this."

The man is too swept away in his rant to notice the hand slipping into his discarded briefcase and coming out with an ID card.

"Sorry," Jorge says. "Really. You can have free coffee for a week. I promise."

The man's eyes narrow as he evaluates Jorge's weary appearance and sporadic personality.

"Okay. Deal," the savvy man says as he walks away.

Jorge wastes no time and flags down a passing cab and gets in. "Take me to the Rings," he commands.

The entire open area outside of the Rings and all side streets are packed with people cheering and celebrating the day they have long awaited. Jorge studies the everyday people he must try to save from the machine they worship. Dressed in smart trousers and a black jumper, Jorge tries to walk and act with a persona of self-importance, just like any other employee of the Rings. No doubt they would be basking in the attention they are about to receive, but Jorge can't let them get this attention. Not when there are lives at stake.

Security guards line the front of the single multistorey building attached to the back of the Rings. The temperature under his collar quadruples as Jorge flashes one of the guards a smile and swipes the stolen ID card on the terminal. Sweat gathers on his forehead as the terminal pulses blue and, after what seems a lifetime, eventually turns green. The gate opens, and Jorge walks through and around the corner.

The growing feeling of dread and displacement has

never felt so strong. Jorge knows this is the right thing to do. The feeling is telling him something, and he has to believe he's translating it right. If the mission is a success, then it will only be he who has to suffer, but if the mission fails, then it will be everyone who pays the price.

Jorge stops to examine a wall map, rolling his finger along the corridors until he finds Main Terminal. "Dammit," he says, realising the terminal's position is centre stage in the middle of the Rings' configuration on a small floating platform.

"Are you lost?" comes a woman's voice from behind him.

Game over, Jorge thinks as he turns to see his capturer. The woman spots the ID card hanging around Jorge's neck.

"Oh, you work here. Sorry, I thought you snuck in or something. Protesters go to any length these days."

"Reading a map. The telltale sign of a new recruit." The pair share a light chuckle.

"I've got to run," says Jorge. "Big day." Jorge leaves the woman, walking in the opposite direction, and once she is out of sight, he runs to the levi-lift marked on the map.

Closed identical doors appear evenly along the corridor, uniform like a beehive. Every surface is metallic, shining from the white lights stretched along the wall. Cautious of passing the wrong place at the wrong time, Jorge reads the room signs as he passes them. Team Room #14, Engine Surveillance, Quantum Engineers, Dr Jenner's Office. Jorge skids to a stop before passing the open door to Dr Jenner's office. Voices come from within. Jorge listens in on the private meeting.

"Not only years of work from past generations, but years of our own work. I won't stop the machine and have it count for nothing."

Jorge gathers that this woman heading the meeting is the lead scientist, Dr Jenner herself. A tall woman with fiery hair and a hotter personality.

Another scientist speaks. "In the light of the new information and expressive concerns from parliament, we need to postpone the experiment. Not stop, but reevaluate."

"I don't care," Dr Jenner shoots back. The argument between the two academics is fierce enough for no other scientist in the room to enter. "It is like there is a compulsion telling me to turn it on. Time travel is finally within reach. You won't stop me, and neither will anyone else. What do citizens with IQs of less than a hundred know about the experiment that I do not?"

"And that is all it is, an experiment. A challenge undertaken in the pursuit of science. If there is a chance that something will go wrong, then we need to call it off. We have already gained so much from the Rings. It won't be a failure. You won't be a failure."

Jorge has heard enough to know he's doing the right thing. The Rings mustn't run today. Jorge tiptoes across the open door and comes to the end of the corridor, where he presses the button for the levi-lift. It arrives with swift speed, and Jorge enters the metal box. He presses the touch screen, and the levi-lift stops at its destination: the Main Terminal.

The doors open onto a magnificent sight. For the first time Jorge is inside the Rings. It's like he's flying on a glass elevator. Rooftops lay leagues below, and the tips of skyscrapers stand at eye level. The central ring wraps around the location. The main terminal is fixed on a platform a short distance from Jorge, no physical pathway connecting it. It looks as if Jorge is floating alone like one of the Rings.

Jorge is in awe of the force field holding his weight, but cannot fight the natural urge to pat the invisible floor with his foot. He looks down to the thousands of people many storeys below as the levi-lift returns to the lower grounds.

Jorge inspects the terminal up close. The computer is embedded in a large desk-like structure with a projecting pole standing tall, supporting a broad ring. He pushes keys on the computer. A message reads: Access Locked.

Jorge reaches for a compressed baton from his pocket and slides it open. He plants his feet firmly and begins to rally a set of blows into the computer. A repeating alarm sounds. Sparks shoot from gashes scraped across the console. Jorge hits more dents into the tough metal encasing the wires he needs to snap. Like a bird breaking the bark off a tree, Jorge grasps a metal sheet in his hands and bends it. A pair of hands grab Jorge and throw him to the ground. He looks up from the bleeding cuts on his hands and sees Dr Jenner.

"What do you think you're doing?" she shouts. "You maniac!"

"I have to stop the machine from turning on!"

"You have no right! Security are on their way. You'd better hope it still runs, or the police won't be the people dealing with you."

"You can't stop me," Jorge whispers before swiping away Dr Jenner's legs and making for the console. He manages to pull away the metal sheet. Blood from his wounds drops onto the console, and he breaks a bundle of wires before Dr Jenner is once again upon him. He's ready this time and dodges a punch, but not the second one. The levi-lift arrives.

"It's over," shouts Dr Jenner. "Security is here." The pair look towards the levi-lift, waiting for the doors to open, releasing a well-trained task force ready to take down any threat. Instead, a banging comes from within the levi-lift, and muffled voices shout. Jorge laughs.

"You removed the console from the mainframe," Dr Jenner says weakly.

Jorge pushes Dr Jenner hard, causing her to fall from

the platform. She lands with force, smacking her head against the invisible floor. Without stopping to think, Jorge grabs a handful of wires and tears them away from their home. The circle frame above the console flashes to life, and a portal appears. The Rings make a clanking sound. Jorge stops still in fear.

The Rings burst to life, and a stream of energy comes from one of the rings, through the console ring, and onto the other ring. A deafening clank, then a bang and a hum. The light is blinding. Raw energy rips through the air. Jorge smells the ooze of burning time and the sizzling of existence.

"You idiot!" Dr Jenner stands behind Jorge. "It won't work properly. You've killed us all!"

"No… no." Jorge is stunned. "I-I saved us all. I had a vision. I had to stop you. You were going to kill everyone!"

A second burst of energy shreds across the Rings with a shockwave that forces Jorge and Dr Jenner to the floor. An all-encompassing white light blurs their vision. Jorge clasps his pounding head, fearing that it might explode. After what feels like an eternity, the light stops, and the Rings go silent.

Jorge and Dr Jenner slowly stand. There is no longer any noise coming from within the stuck levi-lift. In fact, there is no noise at all. The pair survey the world outside. Everything outside the Rings – birds, planes, people, levibikes, and clouds – has stopped frozen.

"It's stopped," says Dr Jenner.

"What has?" replies Jorge, his head still ringing.

Dr Jenner stands in silence as she surveys the world outside, her mouth moving as it tries to form words. "Time," she eventually manages. Without looking towards Jorge, Dr Jenner walks to the levi-lift and presses the door button. Nothing happens. "Why? Why? Today was going to be a good day." Dr Jenner collapses against the levi-lift and slides down the doors as Jorge mumbles to find an answer.

Jorge doesn't really understand what just happened. Is this a nightmare? Or has he just created one? He has to have done the right thing. The signs and the constant feeling had to mean something.

"I was wrong," Jorge finally replies. "The feeling. It was a warning. It wasn't telling me to destroy the Rings. It was telling me to stay away."

Emotion returns to Dr Jenner in the form of rage as she charges over to the console and jams buttons. The computer is unresponsive, "Work dammit!" She shouts as she hits it harder, her anger giving her extra strength. A burst of light fires forth from the console and into every cell of Dr Jenner's body, shredding DNA and then atoms themselves. The light fades, and Dr Jenner has vanished.

Jorge's knees give way, and he flops into a pile of misery. "No, no, no." Jorge looks back to the world in stasis outside. His lip begins to tremble when the levi-lift suddenly makes a noise, signalling its arrival. The doors open to reveal a white portal.

"W-what?" Jorge stammers.

Jorge moves to the portal. The white configuration of particles, a transcendental dilemma solidified, twists in on itself in an infinite loop. Jorge's face inches away, yet unaffected by its pull. He paces the room as he questions the reality around himself, hating himself for what he has done. He looks at the frigid civilians below. His vision fixes on a couple hidden among the crowd of thousands of spectators, frozen forever. The couple are kissing, their love everlasting.

Jorge thinks aloud, "What have you got to lose? You're dead either way, and maybe you deserve that."

He returns to the portal, his frame turned into a silhouette against the white light. He takes a step forward.

Possibilities

Jacob has never fully understood the yearly festivities of Christmas. Even when he was a child, he questioned whether Santa Claus was real before anyone else his age had the inclination of an inquisitive mind. In contrast to Jacob is his wife, Shirley, who is a Christmas fanatic. Shirley loves everything Christmas, especially the post-Boxing Day sales when garden centres sell their leftover seasonal stock with a marked-down price of at least 70%, relieving the shared bank account of Jacob and Shirley from some of the strain of December's onslaught.

Being married to someone you love means compromise, and since it is the first day of December, Jacob's compromise has come. His son, Mart, won't be home from university for a couple of weeks, so it is Jacob's sole burden to heave the eight large boxes of decorations and two Christmas trees down through the small loft hatch. A gap that somehow manages to shrink year by year.

This annual tradition has come to be part of Jacob's calendar of anxiety. Halloween brings with it the dread of strangers knocking at your door. With Valentine's Day arrives high expectations and the inevitable let-down. Christmas appears with a whole bombardment of trouble. The pressure of finding the perfect gift and the need to put on a convincing act when you're given a poor one. The rush for perishable vegetables on the lead-up to the big day when supermarket shelves become bare, and customers morph into their true goblin selves.

The list goes on, but Jacob recoils from reading it.

He understands how Christmas can bring joy, but curses that it must be he who will open the hazardous loft hatch, climb the wooden ladder showing early signs of woodworm, navigate dust-ridden terrain, and play a balancing game as he hauls boxes of overloaded decorations across a perilously unstable-looking floor. His less than unbefitting physique has been made worse through years of worrying. He questions if he will survive to the end.

Jacob pulls the rusted light chain, and a 60-watt bulb (which only reaches 30-watts) flickers from its slumber, illuminating enough of the dark crummy loft for Jacob to be able to complete his arduous task. He sanitises his hands for good measure before pulling on a pair of heavy-duty work gloves and climbing into the loft.

Large boxes are stacked around the chimney column in the centre of the room. Planting his feet firmly in an example good enough for a Health & Safety manual, Jacob pulls the first box towards the loft hatch one carefully planned step at a time. His infrequent visit has disturbed thick dust layers all around him, some catches his nose, and he lets out a loud sneeze. Being a hardened veteran of such ventures, Jacob produces a waiting tissue from his pocket and uses it sparingly. Back to work, he lowers the hefty box down the hatch, resting it on his head as he descends the ladder. Once down, he opens the box to inspect its contents. Everything is still wrapped in bubble wrap from the year before.

More boxes and more perilous journeys. When moving the heaviest of boxes, something breaks, and Christmas tat spills out. Items roll along the floor fashioned from disused doors and out down the loft hatch, saving Jacob the job of throwing them there himself. Jacob inhales a deep breath and asks the empty room, "Why?" as he puffs the air back out. He grumbles while he finishes clearing up the mess and comes down the ladder. He is careful to inspect every spilt item for fear that his wife will find one broken.

As Jacob climbs the ladder to retrieve the last box, he spots a spider on his hand and panics, throwing it off him and releasing his grip from the ladder. His body tilts back, and his balance is threatened, but he throws out a frantic arm and grabs the ladder, steadying himself. One of the steps breaks, but Jacob holds tight. He was right about the woodworm and swears to inform everyone he knows about the dangers of it.

Jacob pokes his head into the loft and surveys for further threats. The coast is clear. He makes his way to the final box, crouches so as not to bump his head on the low ceiling rafters, and moves the box from its resting place against the chimney column when a glowing green light reveals itself. Jacob covers his eyes with an arm from the change in light and jumps back as he does so, hitting his head against a timber rafter. Stunned in more ways than one, Jacob removes his arm. The source of the vibrant light is hidden behind the last box. Jacob cautiously shifts the box with the tip of his shoe, exposing a swirling circle of plasma.

"A portal." Jacob gasps.

"But why?" he thinks. "How?" he tries to figure out. Jacob scratches his head and itches his prickly chin. Still no answers come to him.

Jacob notices that there is an off/on switch next to the portal. He turns over the portal and all its hypothetical and metaphysical meanings in the tumble-dryer of his mind. He is as baffled as a man with average intelligence can be. There is no way of telling what lies through the portal and what of the many possibilities may present themselves if he was to jump in. Forget about excitement, free will and hope, possibility only brings the wrong choice, uncertainty and stress. After weighing up the odds, Jacob has decided what he must do.

With an expression of simple mundane plainness, he switches the portal off, struggles when lowering the last box out of the loft, closes the hatch, and walks away. Jacob has no need for portals. He is content with life on the planet as it is, and no amount of intergalactic excitement can change that opinion. After all, if one crummy old loft can present so much danger, think of all the dangers that a galaxy full of questions could throw at him.

Release

Trodden snow rests on a suburban street. Seamless white clouds mirror the ground's colour. Cars move cautiously over the road's slushy surface. A father walks along the path beside his fourteen-year-old son dressed in a secondary school uniform.

The pair come to a crossing. The father waits, but the son moves on. A car turns the corner, heading for the son, when the father grabs his hand, stopping him from entering the path of the vehicle.

"Careful," the father says.

"I know," replies the son.

The father notices the son recoiling his gloved hand and asks, "What's wrong?"

"Nothing."

"You shouldn't pull away when someone is reaching out."

The son looks both ways and crosses the clear road, the father walking at his side. They walk in silence for a while before an idea comes to the father, and he mischievously slows his pace and crunches a snowball into shape. He lands a light shot on the back of his son, who immediately turns and shouts, "Stop it! I get enough of that at school!"

The father looks down in shame before concern crosses his face. "What do you mean? Are you being bullied?"

"I-I… yes. I get milkshakes thrown at me. Put into bins. The small target is the easiest target. I do nothing to upset them and say nothing after it happens, and they still won't leave me alone."

The father's face is as pale as a ghost as he listens to his son. He replies, "I've been where you are. The ridicule of an entire school."

The son turns and continues a brisk walk. The father paces to catch up.

"It's true. I have. I was bullied until I made it stop."

"Stop how? I'm not going to fight back. That's not the kind of thing I do."

"I didn't say anything about violence. I gained respect. Nothing major. I wasn't held high or feared, but I gained enough so that they liked me. I joined some clubs, found out what interests they had, and pretended to like them as well. Conversation replaced confrontation. It wasn't quick, but eventually the bullying stopped."

The father and son arrive at the school's gate.

"So, what do they like?" asks the father. "The bullies?"

"Football, I guess. They support Arsenal."

"Then tell them you hate Tottenham. Trust me. It'll work a treat."

The son rolls his eyes. "I'll give it a go."

The son turns to enter the school when the father calls to him, "Hey! If they carry on, tell a teacher. Love you."

"Love you too, Dad."

The father watches his son join the mingling crowd of

children, some hurrying for a day filled with tantalising knowledge, others trailing behind for a day of torture.

A light drizzle of rain falls on every inch of exposed surface, bringing out the grey tones of the pavement in abundance. The father waits at the painted green front gate of a small suburban house. His son, dressed in jeans and a jacket, exits the house and walks towards him. Puberty has morphed the young child's face into something more rigid, akin to the realm of teenagerhood. Youth spreads across his face in the form of acne. A growth spurt has put his eye level only a couple of inches below his father's.

"Good morning," says the father. "Ready for a day of learning?"

"As always," replies the son sarcastically.

"Did it work?"

"Did what work?" enquires the son with his brow crossed in confusion.

"Did you gain their respect? Did they stop bullying you?" The father's voice is fast.

"Oh. Yeah. That ended years ago; although they were never nice to me, they did stop teasing me."

"Ah. Of course." The father feigns a futile attempt at understanding.

"Besides" – the son twists his toes into the ground as he looks to the sky – "I haven't seen them since I started sixth form."

An awkward silence flows between the two as something that should be said is left unspoken. The son finally speaks. "I'd best be getting off."

The son goes to move on before the father cuts in with, "Do you mind if I join you?"

The son thinks, his lips almost forming the word no. Instead, he answers, "Sure."

As the son moves past his father, the smell of aftershave glides into the air. "You smell nice," says the father as he walks beside his son, matching him step for step.

The son faces forward. "You know, none of the other dads still walk their sons to school."

"I can leave if you want me to. I just thought that you needed me is all."

"No, no. Please. Stay. You're probably right." The son looks his father in the eyes. Rainwater flattens the son's hair and descends his face.

The pair walk in unison but for the occasional sidestepping around a puddle. The patter of rain hitting wet surfaces plays its unending melody.

"How's your mother?" pries the father in a low tone.

"She's doing good. Still hasn't met anyone, although I think she may have a crush on the plumber."

The pair chuckle.

"And what about you?" says the father.

"This year is make or break. Exams are around the corner. I passed the mock tests, but I feel like all they did was give me another opportunity to fail, as if I somehow used all my good luck to pass them."

"That's not how things work, son. You have the knowledge, the ability to pass."

The son isn't convinced. A car drives past in the road ahead, hitting a pothole and splashing its watery contents over the pavement. The pair rush to pass the splash zone before another car sends a larger wave up behind them.

The son speaks. "What if I fail? University placements, career prospects, everything gone within a second. What then? How do I correct the mistakes of two years of trying?"

The father sighs. He understands the son's feelings with the familiarity of a lived life. He eventually says, "The future is uncertain. It's scary if you think about it too much, but thinking about it is a choice. You can choose to think of the present and forget what the future may bring. Always remember the future is more likely to bring happiness than misery. That is something you have control over. You have prepared for your exams, and now you will pass them. It's as simple as that."

The son's demeanour relaxes as they arrive at the sixth form's entrance.

"I guess this is goodbye for now," says the son. He looks to his father with longing.

"Goodbye for now," says the father with a hint of pain in his voice.

The father watches as his son turns and joins the hurrying crowd of teenagers eager to exit the rain.

The summer sun shines bright with an invigorating warmth as the father waits outside his son's house. His son closes the front door and says, "Hi, Dad. Hot today, isn't it?" Puberty has completed its journey on the son, giving him a sharp jawline and strong shoulders shaped nicely by his denim jacket.

"Yes," replies the father. "Enough to make you want to dance." The father hops on the spot, clipping his heels together. The two laugh as they walk on.

"What will the day bring for my favourite son?"

"Your only son. Well, it's my final day of sixth form. We'll be getting advice on how to live on campus at university etcetera."

"You got in? You passed your exams?" asks the father with delight.

"Yep. Passed them all," the son says in humbleness with a hint of pride.

"Oh! That is fantastic. I'm proud of you, son. Truly."

They share a smile before crossing the road.

"For the first time in years I'm actually excited for the future. I can't wait to start uni. To meet new people."

"All them parties too, I'm sure." The father nudges his son, who chuckles in response.

They walk on, and the father sneaks a look at his son, who has grown into a handsome young man holding his head with a sense of purpose. The father's face turns grave. A sadness glazes his eyes. His pace slows as he thinks before he stops completely. The son notices his father's absence and returns to him.

"What is it?" asks the son.

"You've grown," states the father.

"Well, yeah. That's kind of what happens."

"No, you've grown." The father speaks quietly as if speaking is too much of a burden. He looks at his son. His confidence grows, and he speaks loudly and proudly. "You're sociable, brave, and prepared for stepping into adulthood. My job as a father is done. It's time for me to let you find your own way. I have to say goodbye."

"No, no, please no." The son begins to break, holding some tears back but releasing others. He turns as his world spins out of control around him. He speaks aloud. "I don't want to lose you again. I might need you again. What if I need you again?"

"I wouldn't be leaving unless I was sure that you would make it without me. You still have your mother. She was always better with this parental-advice thing than me anyway. It's going to be okay."

"I need you, Dad," says the son as more tears line his face in streams.

The father's eyes are wet as he says, "A child will always need their parents, their guardians, and we are always there, just not in person. You are ready to face the world, not alone, but on your own. You can do it. You don't need to be holding onto the past anymore."

"Walk me to the gate," begs the son, "one last time."

"No, you can do this on your own. I love you, and that love will always be with you."

The two figures stand against the glowing urban landscape. The distance between them seems to hold their entire history in its short space. The son jumps to his father and embraces him in a tight hug. The father hugs back harder. They release each other. The father holds his son's hands.

"Goodbye, son," says the father with a large smile.

"Goodbye, Dad," says the son with a pained grin.

As seconds tick by, the father's body begins to fade in substance, becoming transparent when the morning sun rises over a nearby house, hitting him with beams of light, transforming his body into sunlight, which dances merrily into the blue sky. The son holds onto the empty space where his father stood. He sniffs, wipes away his tears, and takes a deep breath before walking towards the sixth-form gate one step at a time.

Highway 72

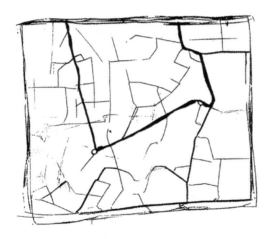

Dane turns his rusting white pickup truck into a petrol station. Driving for twelve hours three days in a row is starting to wear on him, not just mentally but physically. The lack of sleep leaving dark bags under his eyes, ageing him by years. Dane stops the pickup and pulls out a map. He draws a red line from Wiluna to Cue and from Cue to Kalbarri.

Progress marked, Dane leaves his truck. Rain plays metallic music on the thin roof above, and the humid weather wraps around Dane's exposed face. He checks his appearance in the window mirror. He knows he's seen better days, better years, even as he scruffs his hair to do something to change his dismal visage.

Dane studies the building opposite the petrol station. It's old and fashioned like the houses Dane relates to the cheap cowboy TV films he watched as a kid. The building has probably been here since the town's development when gold was discovered nearby in the late nineteenth century.

Dane walks into the small store. A man in his sixties stands behind the counter. He puts down his paper as Dane approaches and places a bottle of soda and a breakfast sub onto the counter. The sub knocks over the soda. The drink fizzes inside the bottle. He will have to wait to open that now.

Dane looks at the clock behind the thin man. It's 9:35. Dane glances out the window. It's too dark for the time of day. The overcast grey weather won't let the sun pass.

"I reckon it's going to stay like this for the week," says the cashier.

Dane looks confused as the cashier scans his items.

"The weather. The rain falls heaviest this time of year. Say, you don't look too healthy."

"We can't all be an Adonis."

"Ain't that the truth." The cashier cackles, exposing his yellow teeth. He wipes back what's left of his starved grey hair. "Why you in these parts, anyway? That's a British accent."

"English, yes."

"Australia's full of English immigrants. I don't mean no offence. Just saying how it is. You here on holiday?"

"Born and raised here. My mother made sure I spoke with an English accent. Carry on the culture, I suppose."

"What brings you out west to Cue?"

"On my way to Kalbarri."

The store owner's face drops serious in recognition of something only he knows.

Dane continues his story, not noticing the firmness of the cashier's stare. "I have a brother who lives by the sea. He's had an operation, needs someone to look after him for a while."

"I appreciate the custom, but wouldn't it have been easier to fly? Most folks fly that way, and those who don't wish they did."

"I-I don't like flying, or heights for that matter."

"What road you taking?"

"Highway seventy-two."

The cashier snaps forward. "Take another way. Don't matter how long it takes. Just do it."

"What? Why?"

"That road's no good. Not for good folk like yourself."

"I'm not one for superstition."

"You won't believe me, but I can't let you pass through here without warning you. Couldn't live with myself if I did that." Working himself into a sweat, the cashier wipes his head with a well-used handkerchief. "Highway seventy-two is a bad place. I don't know the correct word for it. There isn't one to properly describe it. Cursed. Haunted. Supernatural. No, it's something more than that. Anyone who goes down there alone is at risk. You alone?"

"Yeah."

"It only happens when it's raining – I don't know why – and people who are alone don't make it to the other side."

"What are you on about?"

"People report sightings of bodies, many bodies, floating in the sky. You don't want to see them, because when you see them, that means it's happening."

"Wait. I thought you said it only happens to people who are alone. If they see the bodies and are taken, how do you know about them?"

"Dash cam footage. I came across an abandoned car and took it."

"Where's the footage?"

The cashier grows impatient like he's hitting his head against a brick wall. "Some suits came and stole it from me! Thirty-six people in the last four years have come through my doors, not listened. They can't reach you once you pass the valley. Get there and you're safe."

Dane looks the man up and down. "I don't believe you," he says, but his voice tells otherwise.

The cashier slams a closed fist onto the counter. "Fine. I've told you. Done my part." The cashier leaves the counter with a grim face.

Dane stands for a second processing the strange transaction before picking his items up and leaving a ten-dollar note, overpaying for fear of asking for change. He glances back to the cashier as he walks through the door, only to see the man's back towards him.

Seventy miles later, two hundred left to go, and a breakfast sub down. The highway slowly transitioned from an upkept tarmacked road until it degraded into a pothole-stricken hazard. Speed and progress decreased dramatically. Dane examines the map placed over the steering wheel and takes a left turn. A road sign reads "Highway 72".

Dane can see why people are frightened of the road. It looks like it was picked straight from the set of a horror movie. The highway is closer to being a well-made country road. Trees with thick trunks line the dirt road, with an embowing presence. Vision barely penetrates the accompanying canopy of mist. The heavy rain and heat in constant battle. It's mid-morning, and Dane still drives with the truck's headlights on.

The radio fuzzes out of tune and strikes Dane's eardrums with a terrible noise. He pushes the off button a little too hard, causing the knob to fall off. "Blasted thing," Dane complains.

He fixes his focus back on the long narrow road ahead. His attention soon diverts to the light thumps of the window wipers playing a transfixing rhythmic melody.

Throwm-throwm-throwm-throwm-throwm.

His face is expressionless. Suddenly the truck runs into a large pothole and bumps into the air, shaking the large bulk and Dane's skull with it. The bottle of soda spills onto Dane's lap. "Damn it!" Dane shouts as he performs a sharp turn to pull over. The blunt manoeuvre pops a front tire and sends a hubcap rolling into the tree line. Dane slams the brake pedal down, and the truck skids to a halt.

He hangs his head for a second, letting his train of thought catch up with his body before he pats himself down, checking for injuries. A lucky escape. He exits the truck and inspects the damage done to the front right tire. He huffs, then retrieves a car jack, the one spare tire, and a wrench from the bonnet. He laboriously looseness the lug nuts with a hand wrench, places the jack under the frame, and begins to pump the foot pedal. Once the truck is at a reasonable height, he removes the floppy remains of the tire and unscrews the wheel. He chucks the metal wheel onto the back of the truck.

He heaves the spare tire into place, feeling a strain in his shoulder that was not there last year. Dane shoots his head up at the sound of a breaking branch. It sounded as if someone was moving in the trees. Dane begins to attach the bolts with pit-stop speed before calming down and reminding himself that ghost stories are for scaring kids around a campfire. Dane returns to the task at hand and away from his imagination. He attaches an electric pressure pump to the tire and begins to fill it with air.

Click!

The sound of a breaking branch came from the same spot, and Dane's head shoots up faster than before. He stares into the mist. The trees grow larger, and he suddenly feels surrounded.

Click! Click! Click!

Branches snap from left, then right, then all directions. Dane's eyes fire from one place to another, afraid to find something there. Dane realises that he is looking in the wrong place. His body shakes as he slowly turns his gaze upwards to the top of the tree line. The sound of breaking branches grows and multiplies and then… silence.

Dane continues to shake, his breath now quick and

jagged. Small clouds leave his mouth. It should not be this cold. Dane almost slips and looks down, seeing that puddles are freezing over. A live rabbit squirms to free its head stuck in a pool of water in the roadside ditch. The animal's legs kick and scratch at the ice, making no impact before it falls still. Dane's gaze lingers.

Bang! Dane holds his arms above his head in protection against the unknown threat. The spare tire is a shredded mess of rubber.

"Too much air."

Dane surveys the area. Nothing but cold mist in sight. He has no option but to walk back to the petrol station and, if the cashier is to be believed, pray that he makes it there at all.

Dane's walk started with a brisk pace, but after five miles his walk has become more of a tentative shuffle. He is hungry, and his legs ache. He shivers against the cold. "Why is there no signal?" he cries whilst stretching his phone high into the air. "Or a car?" Dane furiously presses random buttons on his phone before shouting and throwing it at the ground. The phone shatters. Dane shuffles past it. The midday sun shines over his head in a white ball above the clouds, its light denied entry to the ground.

Dane is forced to a stop. The noise is back. The noise of breaking branches. Dane tries to ignore it. He shuts his eyes, wills it not to be there. The cracking of branches grows nearer and gathers at every angle. Dane panics and begins to run, adrenaline giving his muscles renewed vigour, waking them from their cold slumber.

As fast as Dane runs, the cracking follows. He trips over his own legs and thuds to the hard ground, sliding along the icy surface that should not be there.

"This isn't real!" he shouts. "This isn't real!" but he cannot hear himself over the sound of breaking branches. He claps his ears under his laboured hands. "This isn't real! This isn't real!" he declares, and it becomes so. The noise stops, and Dane is left listening to his own whimpers.

Dane removes his hands and looks up. Frightened is not a strong enough emotion to describe what he feels. Dane doesn't look away from the forty lifeless bodies floating above the trees, their heads flopping down, looking at him. Blue-hued eyes. Lifeless skin. Wet clothes. Dangling limbs. Even as they come closer, Dane dares not look away. As one, the bodies' jerk their heads to the side. A wolf howl echoes down the valley as Dane's body snaps back over itself. *Crack.*

Unbeknownst

Unbeknownst to Kimona, there is a world she is shutting out. A world that no one notices but is nonetheless there on the edge of our senses. A world she is further closing, glued to her phone, absent from the world she resides in let alone the possibility of another beyond it.

Her phone is a series of miniscule lights on a screen, changing and updating within an instant, forming information as eyes capture its addictive content. Teenage life was complex enough before the strain of keeping up appearances became a twenty-four seven task, following her home from school on her device. An assortment of app notifications flash across the screen, a constant reminder that her attention is required somewhere outside of this room.

Thumbs race to keep up to date with a response, attempting to fill her life with the socialising she is denied at school. She feigns interest in other's lives in the hope that they'll return the favour. They never do. They are as heartless and distant online as they are in the classroom.

No matter what she says, what she does, or how she tries to present herself, she is stuck on the outside, denied access to the tightly formed groups of friends. She is a social circle of one. A dot, awash in the ever-changing sea of high school cliques with their momentary dramas changing the course of alliances and loyalties alike. Nonetheless, she tries to fight the natural flow, faking smiles for the chance that one day she will not be seen as the loser she is told she is, but as someone to talk to, as someone who has something to say.

Kimona lies in bed, her finger swiping upwards along the smooth surface of the screen. A quilt covers her body and drapes over her head, like a shield against the darkness denied the blue light from the phone. Her face an emotionless void as post after post scrolls onto then off her phone's screen.

A notification strikes her ears. Then another. A barrage of messages. Kimona sighs before reading them, her face getting weaker each time before tears form on the edges of her cheeks and wet the pillow below. She reads the spiteful messages, taking in every hate-covered syllable. Baseless accusations claim the most horrid of things. Lies about teachers, fellow students and underhanded deeds.

She types a post but deletes it, knowing that her voice will never be heard. Instead, she reads on. A message reads, "You make me sick. People like you deserve to die!" Kimona's tears turn hot as she squeezes her phone until her fingers go numb.

She lies alone. Dim blue light plaguing the black room. Oppression turns her thoughts into her haters' most dangerous weapon. She closes her eyes and wishes for her life to end.

A soundless movement and a figure appears as a shadow. It moves closer to Kimona. She fidgets as she returns to her phone, causing the quilt to drop slightly. Barely enough light escapes Kimona's cover to reveal a human-like body. It is clothes-less, hairless and has been craving food for weeks. Its pure white eyes shine.

Another silent figure appears and then one more. They move onto Kimona's bed as one, gathering around the unaware girl scrolling on her phone.

The figures' heads move over the crescent of the quilt. The extra light forces definition onto their faces. Sunken cheeks and pointed ears. Their mouths slowly open in unison. Deep toothless holes void of light. A hiss on the cusp of forming a sound. Hands move onto the quilt, clawed fingers clasping the soft fabric. Kimona's brow crosses. The side of her lip rises. Her features fall flat. Her lip trembles, and her eyes look up slowly. So terribly slowly.

Claws drag the quilt back. The phone locks. Light disappears.

Kimona screams as she falls from her bed. Her hands hit the floor, searching for her phone. She finds it and turns its torch on, revealing the figures before her. They stand on her bed, motionless. Their mouths are paralysed as their depthless voices ricochet around the room as they speak as one. "You wish for death. Now death is here."

The figures move towards Kimona as smoke wraps around their bodies, peeling back layers of flesh, revealing their forms beneath. The person in the middle, a teenage girl, wears black leggings and a light grey jumper that flares at the wrists. The boy to the left is tall with long hair and a short beard, dressed like an eighties rocker with a sleeveless denim jacket. The boy to the right has soft features yet to age, blonde hair curling at its edge, and is clothed in matching tweed shorts, blazer, and cap.

Kimona trembles as she watches, waiting for something to happen.

As the bedroom light brightens, the girl steps forward and speaks with a soft voice. "It's okay. We're not here to hurt you. Believe it or not, we hope to do the opposite."

The older boy jokes, "We're not that good at helping ourselves, but we have a bit of a track record at helping others. Okay, that's not exactly true. You're actually my first."

Kimona's mind searches for a logical explanation that could explain what she is seeing. Failing to find an answer, she decides that she must be going mad.

The younger boy says, "You are supposed to explain who we are first."

"Right," responds the older boy.

The girl says, "I was getting there," before rolling her eyes and rejoining her companions. "We were like you." She continues, "We decided that the world had nothing left for us, so of our own accord, we left it. We are now what you call ghosts, and tonight we are here to show you that the world has something left to offer. So please stay in it."

Kimona looks from one ghost to the next, then back to the other. Within an instant, she rushes to her bed and drags the quilt over her, tugging it tight like a fortress.

"Now what?" asks the older boy.

"We wait," says the younger boy.

Kimona stays hidden until the rustling of feet ceases. She waits a few minutes further for good measure before pulling the quilt back and peering out. The room is empty.

The older boy's face appears in the opening. "Hi," he says, causing Kimona to scurry backwards off her bed and onto the hard floor.

"What do you want?" she shouts.

The girl punches the older boy on the shoulder. "That wasn't nice." He rubs his arm as she carries on, "We were alive. Lost, angry, constantly feeling upset in one way or another. Life wasn't easy, but the most dangerous thing to ourselves was ourselves. We were tormented by our own thoughts." The girl looks down with sadness and guilt. "We each took our own lives and became condemned to purgatory."

The younger boy steps forward. "We each made a vow. To guide those troubled souls away from the mistake we committed."

Kimona looks confused. "Who – who are you?"

"The name's Jamiee," answers the girl.

The older boy steps forward and claims loudly, "I'm Lewis."

The younger boy removes his cap, holds it to his chest and says, "Ambrose. At your service."

"You should go back to wherever you came from. Save yourself the hassle and embarrassment. I really don't need any of this. I'm fine."

"That's not how it works," says Jamiee.

Lewis continues, "We can see it in your soul. It's discoloured, fading as your will to live lessens. We can help, if you let us."

Kimona becomes agitated, frustrated that these apparitions don't understand her. She just wants to be alone. "You can't help! You're talking to someone who never feels a hundred percent. Not even ninety, eighty, fifty percent. Some days it's anger. Then there are the days I just don't know how to feel."

Kimona's anger slides into something softer. She looks down with a blank expression as she speaks. "It's a strange state to be in. Surely, you should just *feel* how you're feeling, right? Instead, you find something to pass away the time until you fall asleep, hoping that tomorrow won't leave you feeling so, so bland. But it doesn't change. It's hopeless."

Kimona sits on the edge of her bed.

Jamiee says, "There's always hope. Pain tries to hide it. It tells you that it isn't there, but it is." She sits next to Kimona. "The moments of wellness can be few, and the moments of clarity fewer and shorter. This can change though. Sometimes you have to blow away the clouds to see the sun."

Kimona looks to Jamiee. She sees the sincerity in her eyes. Eyes that have seen their serving of misery. Eyes that she can relate to. She releases her frustration as a huff and asks, "If this is not a dream, if I have not lost my mind, if you are truly real, ghosts on my bed saying that they can help me, what is it that you can do that is so wonderful you think it can help? I have changed schools nearly every year. I am no stranger to false promises."

Jamiee stands and moves in front of Kimona. "Take my hand," she says as she offers it palm up to Kimona, who looks on with a confused expression before making contact with Jamiee's sorrowful eyes.

Kimona slowly raises her hand towards Jamiee's. When they touch, white light appears from thin air, growing brighter until it is all that is visible. Light fades, and a dark scentless smoke fills Kimona's vision.

The smoke parts, revealing another world, almost complete in its detail, yet missing the essence of light. She's in someone else's bedroom. There's a figure, no, a woman, walking towards a table. Judging by her appearance, she would be called alive, yet there is something sullied about her, as if something untouchable has left her body long ago.

Kimona approaches the woman with doubtful steps.

As she raises a hand to her slouched back, the woman whips around, revealing dark holes where her eyes should be, her mouth open in a scream as she falls forward and through Kimona. Kimona screeches as she backs away.

Jamiee stands in the corner of the room with a faceless expression, her features offering no comfort. The door opens, and Jamiee enters, only this Jamiee has black voids where her eyes should be. She rushes towards her mother and helps her to stand.

"This is me," Jamiee pronounces in a voice as quiet as a prayer. "My mother had been poorly for as long as I can remember. When I got old enough to look after myself, I looked after her."

The scene changes around Kimona and Jamiee as smoke whisks in a soundless flurry until it parts with a rush of wind, revealing a new setting. The pair stand in a dim bedroom lit only by the sliver of daylight dragging itself into the room from the gap around closed blinds. The vision of Jamiee tries to make her mother drink from a glass of water. Yellow artificial light expands into the room as the bedroom door creaks open. The outline of a figure in the doorway is revealed by a shadow, the owner's face hidden by the absence of adequate lighting.

"My father," Jamiee says, "forever watching me, not watching over me. Never feeling it was his responsibility to care for my mum, but quick to offer his judgement on how I did. I could never do anything right in his eyes. The feeling of being watched wasn't just at home."

Jamiee turns and walks towards a wall. Kimona hurries to keep up with her as the wall turns into smoke and re-forms as another scene. The pair stand at the front of a classroom. Students aged sixteen scatter on chairs and atop of tables. Each with a companion of some sort, excluding the vision of Jamiee.

Kimona can't stop looking at their eyes, or the absence of their eyes. They draw her attention like something that shouldn't be looked at. Staring at them for too long makes her feel an unnatural fear. She turns away, asking Jamiee, "What is this place? Their eyes. Are they in pain?"

"These are memories," answers Jamiee. "A vision of the past. The year 2009 to be exact. They are not alive, even less so than myself. They are soulless. No more real than the mist that forms them."

"I don't understand," Kimona says as she takes a step further away from the students and closer to Jamiee.

Jamiee continues her story. "Like you, I was alone. People just never seemed to like me. I don't know why. Being a carer made me different to everyone else, I guess. It gave them something to use against me."

A student walks up to the vision of Jamiee, who is absent, staring into blank space. The student pretends to trip and spills her drink over Jamiee, who stands in shock before running out of the room, sobbing.

Kimona goes to run for the girl when Jamiee steps in front of her. "These are the things that have been done. They cannot be undone."

"Then why do you show them to me?" questions Kimona with a rushed voice. "What wicked game is this?"

Jamiee studies Kimona's face. A confused face on the borderline of tears. "Come with me," she commands as she turns, forcing the room to change back into her mother's bedroom. With drawn blinds, the room is lighter. The vision of Jamiee kneels beside the bed. Tears fall from the black holes of her eyes. Jamiee's father steps into the room. He's a tall, large man.

"My mum died," Jamiee says in a voice seeming so far away. "He blamed me for it." Jamiee turns away in preparation of what is to come. Her father runs towards the girl sobbing on the bed. As he raises his foot, Kimona runs towards the helpless girl, but it is too late. His foot is brought down onto her. As it makes contact, the girl is squished, turned back into smoke, along with the entire scene. Kimona and Jamiee stand in an empty darkness.

Kimona breaks the silence, saying in a voice that echoes in the nothingness, "These are horrible things to see. I dread to ask. What happened to you?"

Jamiee looks to Kimona. Her gaze is caring, but strong. Kimona looks away as Jamiee speaks.

"Everyone, everything, had its demand. Some way of pulling at me for attention, draining energy. Once my mum died and my father, well, he… well, it got worse. Some days, it was as if I were powered on thought alone. There was no me, no emotion. The logical side took over and got me from A to B. Is that living?"

Kimona goes to answer, but Jamiee raises a hand, asking for silence. She complies, letting Jamiee continue.

"I just wanted to be comfortable again. To relax again. I thought that the only way to get that was to stop it all, so that's what I did."

As Kimona reflects on the past, she is brought back to the present as her own bedroom returns around her. She rushes to her bed, probing it with her hands. Reassured of its solid matter, she sighs in relief.

"*You* is just one thing your mind does," says Jamiee. "There's plenty of other things going on in there if you stop to observe. Some of these things you can control; other things you can only control how to react to them. I wish I had known these things sooner. That I took charge of how I felt. This thing called living, it nags, it's weighty, and it's torment, but it is also free and wonderful. With life you have the power to change. Life is beautiful."

Kimona says, "I agree that there is beauty in life, but not in living it."

Jamiee stands beside Ambrose. She ruffles his hair as they share a supportive smile. She returns her attention to Kimona and straightens her back.

"Ah, question time," Lewis says. "I love this part."

Jamiee leans forward as she speaks, giving her words an appearance of importance. "A man is imprisoned when he's innocent. Yet he doesn't give in to his surroundings. His heart stays pure. How does the man stay pure?"

The question baffles Kimona. It seems out of place, but why should that surprise her? Nothing about this night has resembled any definition of the word normal. "This is ridiculous," she says. "None of this makes any sense. Life is already enough... well... I..." Kimona looks down with grief.

"Kimona," pries Ambrose, "we are here to listen."

Kimona looks to the boy, his eyes begging for her to open up. She shifts uncomfortably and thinks of the correct words to say. Eventually she begins, "Life has become a drag. Where am I meant to be dragging it to?"

She looks to the ghosts, who offer no solution, so she continues, "Even now. I'm not convinced that you're real. I feel like I'm just a voice inside an empty head. Are you just another voice?"

She chuckles to herself. "That wouldn't be a terrible thing. I have my best conversations in my head. They're so much more interesting than what people have to offer."

Lewis steps forward. "That's not true. I once had a wonderful conversation with this one guy. Turned out he was a tester. Tested all sorts of things. Water slides, beds, even dog food. He was an interesting fella."

"I guess that you have something to show me now too?" mocks Kimona as she moves around the room. "That's the gimmick here, I take it? You each show me your distressing past to highlight some sort of profound hidden meaning? Well, I guess that if the only way for this to end is for me to get through it, then just hurry it up."

"This is not something to be taken lightly," says Ambrose.

"I really don't care," says Kimona. "Just get on with it."

"As you wish," replies Lewis, offering her his hand.

Kimona grabs a hold of it, and the pair are transported to a suburban street. The vision of Lewis walks in front of them, his back facing them. Kimona spots that he's listening to a Walkman. Muffled rock anthems can be heard. They move forward to keep up with him.

"At least we're outside," Kimona says with a hint of sarcasm. "Where are you going?"

"Nowhere," replies Lewis. "I went on walks like this when things became too much. It seemed like all I ever did was walk. I hope you've got your hiking boots on." Kimona looks down at her bare feet poking out from her pyjama bottoms. "Because we'll be following this guy for a while. I haven't got the hang of the transportation side of things, this being my first time and all."

Kimona offers her reassurance. "Don't worry about it."

"That's the attitude." Lewis smiles for the first time. It seems like something new to him, something that he hasn't mastered the control of. "How is this your first time? Judging by the Walkman, I would say we're in the eighties. Jamiee is younger than you, and she can do the scary transportation thing."

"You can't help others until you've helped yourself. Not with stuff like this. You have to be ready. Just because you're a ghost doesn't mean you don't have baggage to unpack."

The pair come to a stop behind the vision of Lewis; their progress is halted by a crossing busy with passing cars.

"I guess I should get to it, then," he says. "Tell you my story and all that."

"You don't have to," offers Kimona. "I get the motive by now, and I'm no stranger to the darkness of this world. Believe me."

"These stories are not just about the darkness, Kimona. Darkness cannot exist without light."

The road is empty, and the three resume their walk.

"When I was young," says Lewis, "I was curious. I took pleasure in learning. I read books on everything. All the science and philosophical subjects. However, like you, I was a loner, and with no one to talk to about my thoughts, they spoke to themselves."

"I can relate," says Kimona as she watches the figure in front of her walk with a slouch. "My head gets so confused sometimes, and I just don't know what to think. I hate myself for not knowing myself."

Lewis offers a supportive smile to Kimona, who shies away from it.

"I became depressed," he says, "and this depression turned my knowledge into ammunition. I became disassociated with the world. I never felt that I belonged in this realm. It was as if the atoms that made up my body had no right to develop an emergent consciousness."

The vision of Lewis walks through a puddle. His feet are soaked, but he doesn't seem to notice as he continues walking.

"Am I making sense? I feel like I'm losing you." Lewis rubs the back of his neck, hiding his embarrassment.

"No, you're doing fine. Please continue."

"Good, good." Lewis's voice returns to a sombre manner. "It was as if I had been asking a question my entire life, and I didn't know the answer to it because I didn't know the question. There was too much going on inside this head. No matter how I filled my days, they were never fulfilled. The worst part was that I stayed in it, this life that I so disliked. The thoughts came daily on repeat and going nowhere. I wished they wouldn't make an appearance. So I stopped them."

The vision of Lewis has led them to an entrance to a forest. Its thick canopy sucking all light away from the space beneath it. The vision of Lewis enters the gloomy mouth of the forest, consumed in its darkness. Lewis and Kimona come to a stop outside.

Lewis turns to Kimona and says, "Trust me. You don't want to end your life, you just want to end the life you're living. I became confused. I needed someone to show me the way out. I'm here to show you the way out of the forest."

Lewis offers Kimona his hand. She gently holds it, and smoke emerges from the mouth of the forest, wisping around the pair. When it leaves, the two are back in Kimona's bedroom, with Jamiee and Ambrose patiently waiting. Ambrose. So young. So pure. Angelic looking in his boyish appearance. What horrors have befallen him? Kimona recoils from thinking further.

Instead, she thinks back to Jamiee kneeling alone on the floor, then of Lewis walking alone in his misery. She holds her head, trying to close off the world around her. She breathes fast and short.

"This is too much. I don't want to see any more. You need to leave me alone." She paces the room. "You are showing me terrible things. You're making things worse. Please, please leave me alone."

Jamiee raises her soothing voice. "The Sagrada Familia began construction almost a century and half ago, yet it's not complete."

Kimona stops. Her brow crosses in confusion as Jamiee asks, "Why do people continue to build?"

"Enough with the riddles!" Kimona's voice drips with spite. "If you have something to say, say it! The world is bad. I know this already."

"The bad is unavoidable," says Jamiee, "but luckily, so is the good. It is just that sometimes you must go through the bad to get to the good."

"Speaking of which," interjects Ambrose, "I am afraid there is one tale left to tell." Ambrose holds up his small hand.

Kimona walks away from the boy. She rests on her desk and whispers, "I don't want to see it."

Ambrose walks to Kimona and takes her hand gently in his own. Dark smoke fills the room. Kimona panics, trying to pull her hand away from his, but his grip is unyielding. The smoke parts, and the pair are standing outside a manor house under a grey raining sky. Servants load luggage onto a horse and carriage. A husband and wife escort their son into the carriage with a brisk pace. Their son looks like Ambrose, only a couple of years younger and without any eyes. He is confused and looks back to the house.

"That is me," says Ambrose. "My father was a successful businessman. A fire in his factory took dozens of men's lives and ours away with it. He lost everything that unfaithful day, including his spirit."

The horse rides towards Kimona and Ambrose.

Kimona steps back in fear as the carriage bounds towards them, but at the moment before it hits, it turns to smoke, billowing outwards and changing the scene around them. They now stand outside an endless row of dull terrace houses under the starry night sky. Candlelight illuminates silhouettes in an upstairs room.

Ambrose continues, "We moved into accommodation fit for a lifestyle we were not accustomed to. As a defeated man, my father turned to drink. He became venomous, his influence turning my mother into a frightful wreck."

Shouting comes from within the house. The silhouette of a man beats a woman to the floor. Footsteps run down the stairs. The front door opens, and Ambrose, now only a year younger than his ghost, runs into the street.

As the young boy races into the distance, smoke travels down the road and towards Kimona. The smoke swaps the road of terrace houses for a bank of the river Thames. White covers the cobblestone streets, and a perpetual mist lies stagnant in the air. This is not the fun white that comes with a fresh layer of snow. This is the deadly kind that arrives with frostbite.

Kimona struggles to see further than a few feet in front of her, but she sees the distant orange glow of lit lamps and hears the sounds of merrymaking. "What is that?" she enquires.

"It will be revealed in time," says Ambrose with plain

honesty. "We were forced into a shared flat. A room fit for one held six. I was placed next to strangers plagued with lice and the flu."

Ambrose looks up to Kimona with his round eyes. "You have moved from school to school your entire life, not settled long enough to readjust to your surroundings. I know this feeling of displacement. Like you, I was comfortable in another life and could not adapt when that life was no longer mine. I had no schooling for the ways of common people. I had none of their inherent will to fight for scraps. I knew not how to provide for myself or how to go about securing employment. I was clueless in the ways of the street, often falling prey to the whimsy of others."

"What about your parents?" Kimona asks with pressure. "Surely, they looked after you."

"They had given up on their own futures; they paid little heed to mine. So I would busy myself wandering the streets of London."

A vision of Ambrose jogs past them and to the side of the river. He looks over its walled edge and down onto the river below. He chuckles happily at the sight.

Kimona joins the vision of Ambrose, peering over the side of the river; they both smile. The river has frozen solid, and an array of market tents and stalls has been erected on its surface. Entertainers of all kinds play music and offer small displays of their talents to the passing crowd.

"I read about this in class," says Kimona. "The frost fair. I always wanted to see it."

The vision of Ambrose looks to the stairway leading down to the fair. A ticket master blocks the way. The boy's smile fades as he turns to Kimona, showing her his absent eyes. His smile returns with an idea, and he runs away.

"It was like a sacred sight," Ambrose says. "The smell of candy floss. The bliss of laughter. A reminder of the things that I had lost. I wanted to be a part of such joy again, so I sneaked down onto the river."

Ambrose walks through the ticket master and down the stairs. Kimona follows, afraid to pass through the man at first; she shuts her eyes and walks through him, forcing him into the smoke he is made from before he re-forms in the position he was in before.

She catches up to Ambrose, watching the vision of himself hurrying from one place to another, taking in the vibrancy of each stall and performer with such vigorous amusement. A fire breather sends a burst of flames into the air, and the crowd cheers. The boy claps. He turns when a strong hand clasps his shoulder.

"Ticket, please," a deep man's voice asks.

The boy makes for the exit, but is cut off by another man. The rogue men drag the boy into the mist of the river, far away from the fair.

Kimona runs for the boy. "Leave him alone!" she shouts.

She enters an area of the river lit only by the solitary street lamp above. She stops dead in her tracks, her hands shooting over her mouth as she watches the men savagely beat the boy.

A blanket of smoke pulls over the scene. It parts to reveal a vision of Ambrose stepping towards a hole in the frozen river cut away for fishing, his empty black eyes staring down into the rushing river beneath. The sound of the fast water growls loudly.

"There were no longer any good days. There were just bad ones and not-so-bad ones. The water seemed free, or at least to offer me some sort of escape."

The vision of Ambrose steps into the hole. As he falls, a splash of smoke exits the hole and fills all that Kimona can see. She holds her face, sobbing hard. When she finally removes her hands, she is back in her own bedroom, with Ambrose, Jamiee, and Lewis watching over her.

"You were only a boy," she says. "You shouldn't have been in that position."

"Yet you dare to do the same," replies Ambrose. "I made a mistake. Gone was the day, and so too the opportunities along with it. Opportunities for the same laughter, love, and warmth I missed. Why deny the possibility for them if you long for them so dearly?"

Kimona surveys the three ghosts. Jamiee with her caring eyes, Lewis with his slight grin, and Ambrose with his innocence. She wonders, if these kind people could not make it, what hope does she have?

Jamiee goes to speak, "A woman—" but Kimona cuts her off, standing tall and shouting, "I didn't ask for this! You don't understand. You can't help me. I'm a lost cause. I like few things and want to do even less. My feelings are all processed the same. Joy, sadness, anger. It doesn't matter how I feel, they all have the same dull taste."

Kimona steps away from the ghosts. "I get a sense of a feeling, but not enough to call it an emotion. It's like feeling the effects of an emotion, but not the emotion itself. As if feeling the heat from a fire yet being blind to the flames."

She raises her hands in defiance. "You show me the pain of living, yet ask me to continue. If this was the job you set out to do, then well done."

Kimona looks to the ghosts, begging for them to speak, yet they stand silent. She falls onto her bed. "Without a choice these thoughts come with me everywhere. If only there was a drawer to store them in. An out-of-mind forgotten-about place where important things and trivial worries rub shoulders in the darkness of a hidden somewhere. But no. My thoughts come with me everywhere."

Kimona drags herself under the quilt of her bed. "Once you leave me like everyone else, I will resume where I left off."

Minutes feel like hours as Kimona waits under the

shelter of her quilt for the ghosts to leave. Their presence made aware by the occasional ruffle. Eventually, Jamiee pulls back the quilt and lies next to Kimona, who takes no notice of the girl and looks down in sorrow. Jamiee waits beside Kimona.

Time passes without a word until Kimona eventually says, "I'm sorry that you have wasted your time with me."

"We're not finished yet," Jamiee says with a slight grin. "Did you think it would be that easy?"

Kimona gives a light chuckle.

"There is still one question to ask. A woman has a loving family, a prosperous career, and good health. Why does the woman weep?"

Kimona ponders the question. Unable to contrive an answer, she admits defeat. "Why have you asked me these questions?"

Jamiee smiles warmly as she speaks. "A man wrongly imprisoned stays pure, we continue to build the Sagrada Familia, and a woman with everything still weeps. The answer to all three questions is the same. It is because we hope for tomorrow. A man stays pure through his hope for being reunited with those who believe him. He wants to stay pure for them, so he makes it so. We hope for a better future filled with things of marvel, so we build it."

Jamiee's smile slips from her face. "The truth cannot be hidden. Hope does come with a cost. There is the chance that things won't go to plan. Hope can be painful. A woman with everything will weep because she fears to lose everything. Fear is the flip side of hope. The key is not to forget that hope is there when it is out of sight."

Kimona studies Jamiee's sincere words. For the first time, she admits to herself that there may be a place of hope, even if it is the smallest of places. She removes her quilt and stands.

"The entire future plays in my head. All of what I want it to be and all of the infinitely possible wrong turns along the way. How am I meant to face that? How am I meant to see the one hopeful path when it is easier to be removed from the equation?"

Lewis says, "Do you know what you would miss if you were not here? Life. The beauty of possibilities. They can be scary, but, boy oh boy, what a marvel they can be too."

Jamiee stands in front of Kimona. Lewis and Ambrose close in around her, forming a tight triangle. They reach up and hold onto each other's hands. A yellow nimbus begins to emanate from their connection. It grows brighter as the world begins to spin. Kimona turns, looking for a way out that is not there. She breathes out and stands still. She takes refuge in the ghosts' presence and opens herself to whatever they have to offer.

The world outside the triangle is white light. Clumps of smoke appear with visions played out on them as if from a projector screen. Scenes of Kimona's possible futures unfold as they spin around her. Dozens of scenes of laughter, friendship, and love. Lazy weekends reading. Standing at the top of a mountain with the view of the entire world below. Kisses shared under a sparkling sky. Holding a baby boy in her arms. Shock hits Kimona like a wrecking ball as raw emotions are reawakened.

More smoke screens appear, uncountable in their number. Displays of joy stand side by side with scenes of sorrow and pain, but laid out here one after another, Kimona can see that there cannot be one without the other. Failure and heartbreak lead to resilience. Falling down means that you can get back up. Sorrow brings out the shine of elation. In one scene her mother passes away from sickness, and in the next she is running in a marathon, raising donations for a foundation that goes on to cure the disease. Life and all of its intricate ramifications are given meaning by being joined together.

Kimona looks from screen to screen. Sadness and happiness, returning to her like long-forgotten friends as she sees the possibilities her pain denied her. By seeing them, she can hope for them to come true. She looks to each of her ghostly companions.

"Thank you," she says to Lewis.

He nods his head in response before fading out of existence. Kimona goes to protest, but Ambrose begins to fade. She goes to raise a hand to him when he removes his cap and bows in response before disappearing.

Kimona turns to Jamiee. The pair share a smile. Tears edge around Jamiee's face.

"What now?" asks Kimona.

Jamiee says, "Choose to live. The possibilities are endless," as her body fades and her final words drift into nothing.

The world stops spinning, and the smoke screens disperse one by one, leaving Kimona alone in her bedroom. Their images still bright in her mind, tears of joy bring pain to Kimona as she rejoices at the divine threads that life uses to weave its tapestry. Each emotion offering a different colour, creating a rainbow of experience. She sighs in relief as her forgotten smile beams like a summer morn.

Sombre Days

Snow covers the ground in a smooth sheet of white. Anything underneath it hidden from sight. The rising sun shines through the morning mist. I walk over the unbroken surface, leaving nothing to show that I am here to exist.

I long for a body, a way to touch, yet I struggle to accept it as such. I hear and see the world I left behind. The world I departed by no choice of mine.

I am lost. I pass like the morning frost.

Then it is night. Try as I might, time no longer travels right. I walk through an empty field. Faceless crop. No one in sight, not a single light.

My constant walk is endless. I yearn to rest. I beg my legs to stop, but this is a command I no longer possess. I tell them to stay, to possibly slow, yet their perpetual motion continues to go.

Drifting has brought me back to where I began. Parents hold an infant at the start of their lifespan. A baby's cry pierces hushed air. I continue to move on to somewhere.

Life is something I cannot reprove and my legs continue to move.

Printed in Great Britain
by Amazon